"The McBain stamp: sharp dialogue and crisp plotting."
— *Miami Herald*

"A master storyteller."
— *Washington Times*

"McBain keeps you reading and keeps you guessing…
The book is a winner."
— *London Sunday Telegraph*

*"Eileen!" he called, unable to contain himself any longer, wanting to wake her, needing the shot now as a man on a desert desperately needs water. This was life and death. This was the difference between being able to breathe, and dying.*

*"Eileen! Wake up, wake up. Help me."*

*He was shivering now, barely able to keep his body steady. He walked rapidly across the room and stooped over the bed.*

*"Eileen!" he said, his voice a hoarse whisper.*

*He reached down and touched her shoulder gently, his fingers trembling. "Eileen. Eileen, snap out of it."*

*He shook her more violently, his lips moving frantically, gulping great gulps of nothing in his throat. "Come on, kid," he pleaded, "come on now, let's go, come on."*

*With a sudden violent movement, he ripped back the sheet, exposing the length of her body relaxed against the whiteness of the bed. His eyes traveled down to the hollow of her navel.*

*He noticed the holes then.*

*They were small holes, just to the right of her navel. They were rimmed with red, and there was a dried river of red across the flatness of her stomach. The redness stretched out beneath her, staining the sheet in gaudy brilliance...*

# So NUDE,
# So DEAD

## *by* **Ed McBain**

A HARD CASE        CRIME NOVEL

**A HARD CASE CRIME BOOK**
(HCC-120)
*First Hard Case Crime edition: July 2015*

Published by

Titan Books
A division of Titan Publishing Group Ltd
144 Southwark Street
London SE1 0UP

in collaboration with Winterfall LLC

Print edition ISBN 978-1-78116-606-2
E-book ISBN 978-1-78329-361-2

Design direction by Max Phillips
*www.maxphillips.net*

Typeset by Swordsmith Productions

The name "Hard Case Crime" and the Hard Case Crime logo
are trademarks of Winterfall LLC. Hard Case Crime books
are selected and edited by Charles Ardai.

Printed in the United States of America

*Visit us on the web at www.HardCaseCrime.com*

*The new ones, the old ones, they're all now dedicated to the love of my life—my wife, Dragica.*

*SO NUDE, SO DEAD*

# Chapter One

There was the jangling, of course. It wouldn't be morning without the jangling. It was as if someone deliberately gathered up every nerve end in his body and tied them together every night. And in the morning—this morning, every morning—he'd sit up in bed with the ache in his body. It was almost delicious, especially when he knew he had the stuff waiting for him. It was painful too, but painful in a sweet way, almost as if the wanting were too exquisite to bear.

God, he needed a shot.

He sat up in bed, the sheet forming a little tent over his bent knees. He was big in a sinewy, leather-thonged way. His shoulders, bare against the backboard of the bed, were broad and muscular. His hair was almost blond, that light shade of brown that streaks gold in the sun. He wore it cut close to his head on the sides, fuller on top. A widow's peak cut into his forehead pointed to a straight nose, a firm mouth and jaw. Only his eyes did not fit the rest of his face. They were gray, recessed deeply on either side of his nose, pocketed in shadow.

They pinpointed with light now as he stared around the room. It was a strange one, but that didn't surprise him. He'd wakened in plenty of strange rooms since he'd been on the stuff. The rooms were all alike, so long as he had a shot waiting. He yawned, covering his mouth with his hand. He was beginning to tremble already.

That was when he noticed the blonde beside him in the bed. Her hair was spread out over the pillow like a golden fan, mist-like, glistening under the rays of the sun that streamed through the open blinds. She was pale, her skin drawn taut over high cheekbones.

He scratched his head. Beneath the jangling that was becoming more insistent in his blood stream, he began to remember. As if to check his memory, he looked down at the girl again.

She had a strong chin, and a neck that swept away from the chin in a smooth, clean line. The sheet reached to just below her breasts. His eyes dropped to her arm, lying over the sheet palm upward.

The marks were there. The marks that looked something like healed burns or old scars. The hundreds of puncture marks, one over the other, blended together into a telltale smear. The addict's coat of arms. Yes, this was the girl, all right.

He looked down at his own arm, his eyes fastening on the identical marks. Again the revulsion seized him, the knowledge that slapped him in the face whenever he saw the marks, or whenever he looked into his eyes in a mirror. And yet, in spite of the revulsion, there was anticipation as he stared at the needle scars.

*Somewhere in this room, there were sixteen ounces of heroin.*

He swung his legs over the side of the bed, careful not to disturb the girl. Sixteen ounces of heroin! His tongue ran over his lips excitedly, as he thought greedily of the drug. He would wait, yes, he would hold it off until the need grew unbearable. But first he would find it, get it all ready for when he really needed it, when he couldn't stand it any longer.

He put on his pants, excited now at the thought of teasing himself, pleased because he knew the stuff was waiting for him. And a cold analytical part of his mind told him he was behaving like a fool. *Yes, yes, he knew that, dammit. He knew it.* He shut his mind to the glimpse he'd had of himself. He glanced at the girl on the bed. Man, she was really out. How much of the stuff had they taken last night?

He tightened his belt and began thinking of the events that led to this moment.

*He was sitting at a table. Yes, he remembered that quite well. What was the name of the place? Johnny's? No, he hadn't been to Johnny's since… Ace High, that was the name. It was late, and she was singing. She sang well, sort of deep and throaty, from way inside her. She wore a long-sleeved blouse and he remembered wondering why she covered her arms—the addict looking for another addict, the blind seeking the blind. Christ, how had he gotten into this? What had happened to the guy he used to be? Where had he lost himself?*

He opened a door, discovered a closet, and walked to another door on the opposite side of the room. It was the bathroom, and he walked inside, turned on the hot water and let it run for several moments. At the back of his mind was a thought that sent shivers of anxiety down his back. Heroin.

*"You're cute," she said. She was slightly looped, he thought, and her voice sounded deep and throaty even when she spoke. "I noticed you while I was singing, and I said to myself, He's cute. I was right." She looked better close up, much better than she did on the bandstand. She had her hair pulled back tight over her ears, clipped at the back of her neck with an amber clasp, fanning out over her shoulders. The blouse she wore had a deep V sweeping down from her shoulders, terminating in a shadowed cleft between high breasts. He remembered staring at the soft whiteness of her skin as she leaned over the table.*

*"You're very cute," she repeated, and he said, "You're not bad yourself."*

*She blew smoke across the table. "Sparkling dialogue," she said dryly. "Refugees from a Grade-B stinkeroo."*

*"Pardon me. I'm not dressed for repartee."*

*"It doesn't matter, sweetheart. You'd be cute if you spoke Burmese."*

*"Thanks. You're not bad—"*

*"I know. I know. I'm not bad myself."*

*They laughed then, and she covered his hand with hers on the table.*

He dried his face with a towel he found in the bathroom. There was lipstick on the towel and the words "Hotel Stockmere" in blue script embroidered in the left-hand corner. It was almost time. He was really beginning to need it. His hands shook as he replaced the towel on the rack. It was time to start looking for the stuff. Let's see, where had they put it?

*"What's your name?" she asked, gripping his hand tighter.*

*"Ray."*

*"That's all?"*

*"Ray Stone."*

*"Eileen Chalmers." She squeezed his hand again. Then she looked up into his face, her mouth unsmiling, "When did you get your last fix, Ray Stone?"*

*He looked at her suspiciously. "I don't know what you're talking about," he said.*

*"Don't you?"*

*"Not the faintest idea."*

*She pulled her hand back across the table, her fingers moving to the small pearl button on her left sleeve. Deftly, she undid the button and shoved the sleeve back abruptly. She held it up only long enough for him to see the marks. Then she pushed the sleeve down and fastened the button again.*

*"I thought girls used their legs," he said.*

*"My legs are too nice to mark." She swung her feet out from under the table, pulled her skirt back to the tops of her stockings. He saw the sleek roundness of thigh and calf, the slender ankle. Then the skirt came down again, covering her knees.*

*"See?" she asked.*

*"I see."*

He started searching in the bureau drawers because he seemed to remember her putting the stuff there. The top drawer held his wallet, his cuff links, and a half-empty package of Camels. He closed the drawer and opened the middle drawer. Two towels were neatly folded there. Otherwise, it was empty. His face twitched as he opened the bottom drawer. Empty. He took a deep breath, the demand for the drug growing stronger now, and looked anxiously around the room. Perhaps he should wake her? No, he'd find it. It had to be around somewhere. Sixteen ounces of the stuff didn't just get up and walk away. How many fixes were there in sixteen ounces of pure heroin?

*"I asked about your last fix,"* she said.

*"I heard you."*

*"Well?"*

*"I don't remember. About ten o'clock, I guess."*

*"Man, that's a long time ago."*

*"I suppose so."*

*"How would you like a* real *fix?"*

*"Maybe."*

*"Heroin,"* she said, almost tasting the word.

*"Sounds interesting."*

*"Or aren't you on hero—"*

*"I said it sounded interesting,"* he interrupted quickly.

*She grinned, her lips parting like an opening flower.*

*"You're cute, Ray Stone. Maybe we'll share more than a fix."*

*"Maybe."*

*"This is the last set,"* she said. *"I sing two more numbers. Wait for me, Ray."* She rose, her fingers lingering on his arm. She turned then and walked toward the bandstand, her hips straining against the tight skirt.

He searched the closet frantically. All right, he told himself. All right, this is far enough, I want it enough now, I want it pretty damn bad, I want it very much, too damn much, I need it right now. Where is it? Where the hell did she put it? How much longer does a guy have to stand this? Jesus, how much longer do I have to wait for the day to begin? Where is it? Where did she put it? Sixteen ounces. Jesus, where did it go?

He slammed the closet door in a frenzy and stalked into the bathroom.

*There in her room, they clung together, trembling with the discovery of their bodies, and trembling with the promise of the drug waiting for them.*

*That was when she showed it to him. She opened the bureau drawer and took out a small tin candy box.*

*"Chocolates?" he asked.*

*"Better than candy, Ray. Much better."*

*She lifted the lid, and his eyes opened wide. He looked down, his hands almost reaching for it.*

*"Is—is that—"*

*"That's what it is, baby. Sixteen ounces of it."*

*"Sixteen ounces! Jesus, where'd you get—"*

*"Is it enough, do you think?" She smiled teasingly.*

*"Enough? Jesus, it must be worth a fortune."*

*"We're going to have a real fix, Ray baby. No scrimping this time. We can use all we want. We can fly, baby, we can really build wings."*

*He took her into his arms, kissing her warmly.*

He slammed the door of the medicine chest shut. His hands trembled and there was a lurching pain in his stomach. He scratched his cheek nervously, scratched his temple, scratched his cheek again. In desperation, he looked in the shower stall, found only a bar of soap, threw this against the wall in fury. Where the hell is it? his mind screamed. He scratched his cheek again, not knowing what his hands were doing anymore. The muscles along his back began to quiver. He had to have it! Where was it, damn it, where was it?

*They did it slowly. They measured out only enough of the white powder to give them wings, just enough to blow off the tops of their heads. Not too much. Not the big fix, the lethal dose an addict never woke up from. Just enough to give them a kick, a kick with an iron shoe behind it.*

*Each holding a loaded hypodermic, they walked to the bed, and emptied the syringes into their arms.*

*"Man, this is one big shooting gallery," she shrieked.*

*"The biggest, the biggest," he screamed with her, the drug beginning to take hold.*

*"I'm pulverized! I'm swinging. Man, I'm stoned!"*

*"Flying, flying, flying up there! Man, watch out, watch out for me in my brand-new Cadillac."*

*The Cadillac dream had taken over then, with Ray behind the wheel. That was all he remembered. It had been one hell of a fine fix.*

He went through the bureau again, the closet, the bathroom, even the shower. He went through her purse, scattered her underwear all over the floor, tossed his own clothes off the chair, his shirt, his socks, looking for the elusive candy tin with the white powder in it.

"Eileen!" he called, unable to contain himself any longer, wanting to wake her, needing the shot now as a man on a desert desperately needs water. No kicks this time, no kicks involved at all. This was life and death. This was the difference between being able to breathe, and dying.

"Eileen! Wake up, wake up. Help me."

He was shivering now, barely able to keep his body steady. He walked rapidly across the room and stooped over the bed.

"Eileen!" he said, his voice a hoarse whisper, a light sweat covering his body with a cold film. "Eileen."

He reached down and touched her shoulder gently, his fingers trembling. "Eileen. Eileen, snap out of it."

He shook her more violently, his lips moving frantically, gulping great gulps of nothing in his throat. "Come on, kid," he pleaded, "come on now, let's go, come on."

With a sudden violent movement, he ripped back the sheet, exposing the length of her body relaxed against the whiteness of the bed. He shook her again, and his eyes traveled down to the hollow of her navel.

He noticed the holes then.

They were small holes, just to the right of her navel. They were rimmed with red, and there was a dried river of red across the flatness of her stomach. The redness stretched out beneath her, staining the sheet in gaudy brilliance.

Her shoulders were quite cold.

A horror that was worse than the drumming need for the drug seized him. He realized then that Eileen Chalmers wasn't breathing.

## Chapter Two

He didn't touch anything. He didn't touch a thing, even though his mind told him his fingerprints were probably scattered in a hundred places all around the room.

He backed away from the bed, still trembling from the shock.

So that's what bullet holes look like, he thought. Round and small, and they spill blood over bellies, they kill pretty young girls. He walked back to the bed and pulled the sheet up over her breasts, hiding the ugly holes in her stomach, hiding the blood stains.

"I have to get out of here," he said aloud, surprised at the hoarse sound of his own voice. He bit his lip, set his teeth tightly. That's all the cops would need, all right—a hophead to pin this on. Under the influence of narcotics, Ray Stone, hophead. He washed his hand over his face, trying to wash away the title he'd given himself. But I *am* a hophead, he argued, forgetting the dead girl completely. He had reached the point where he could admit it freely, say it as casually as he would say "I am a boy scout" or "I am an Elk," wasn't that it ? No, no, that wasn't! That wasn't it. He could never say it like that, never. He would always carry the shame, always wonder if it showed in his eyes, always roll up his sleeves only so far when washing his hands, afraid the telltale scars would show.

He remembered the dead girl abruptly. He had to get out of there in a hurry. He had to get out of there, and he had to get a shot before he blew up completely.

A shot.

Several shots, and all pumped into her belly. Why hadn't he heard them? Sure, he'd been blind, but wouldn't the shots have penetrated, wouldn't they have shaken him from his stupor? Or wouldn't someone in the hotel have heard them? Surely someone would have heard the shots.

Unless a silencer were used. And if there had been a silencer on the murder gun, then the killer had come to this room intent on doing murder. This wasn't a question of Eileen's surprising a sneak thief or— *I need a shot, I need a shot!*

Quickly, he picked up his shirt from the floor. He buttoned the shirt rapidly, slipping his tie under the collar and hastily knotting it. He removed his jacket from the back of the chair, shrugged it onto his shoulders. From the bureau drawer he took his cuff links and fastened them at his wrists with trembling fingers.

He took the crumpled package of Camels from the drawer, put one between his lips, and struck three matches before he finally lighted it. When he looked into his wallet, he found it was empty. His mind almost screamed at the discovery.

When would he learn? When would he ever learn? Good God, how could he leave himself wide open like this? The sixteen ounces of stuff, where was it? Hell, he'd been over the room with a fine comb. The stuff was gone, vanished, *poof!*

If he didn't get a shot soon, *he* would vanish, blow up, dry away; dry up, blow away, he meant. He didn't know what he meant. Typical hophead, he thought with disgust. Typical muddled jackass. Leaving himself in this predicament. Leaving himself wide open for the monkey to hop on his back. He bit his lip, clenched his hands together. He wanted to feel sorry for himself, but he couldn't. He had too much pride—yes, pride, damn it— to indulge in self-pity. A strange bittersweet memory of the Ray Stone that used to be crossed his mind, to be immediately stifled by a fresh pang of desire.

He needed money!

What day was it? Saturday? No, it was Sunday. His father would be home. He couldn't call his father, not after all he'd put him through. But he needed money. He could count on his father, he had to call him. Quickly, he walked to the phone on the end table near the bed. He lifted the receiver, held it to his ear, waited.

"Yes?" the crisp voice asked.

He hesitated, wondering if he should answer, wondering if the girl would remember his voice when the cops started asking questions later.

"Yes?" the voice repeated.

"Line, please," he said, trying to keep his voice muffled.

"Yes, sir; just a moment."

He waited until he heard a dial tone, then rapidly dialed, repeating the numbers to himself as he spun the dial, breathing harshly, the pain eating at his insides.

He fidgeted while he listened to the buzzing on the other end.

"Hello."

"Hello, Dad? This is Ray."

"Ray! Where are you? Are you all right?"

"I—I need help, Dad." He felt sick, disgusted at himself for crawling back to his father like a little boy whenever he needed help. His father should refuse. After all the slaps he'd given him, after all the things he'd said, his father should refuse. He waited.

"What is it?" His father's voice was tired. He sounded as if he'd always been tired.

"I'm in a jam, Dad."

There was a long pause, and Ray heard an audible sigh on the line. He knew what his father was going through. He knew, and he hated it. But he needed a shot.

"I won't give you any more money, Ray. Not for that. We've already been over—"

"I don't want any money," he lied. "I just want to talk to you. I'm in trouble."

His father sighed again, the sigh of a man who has taken more than he can bear. Ray listened, and the sound sliced through him like a dagger. "What kind of trouble?" his father asked gently.

"There's a dead girl with me, Dad."

"What?"

"A girl. She's been shot."

"Oh my God!" There was a long silence on the line. "Where are you, son?"

"At a hotel. The Hotel— I—I can't remember." He cursed his muddled mind, cursed the drug.

"Are you downtown?"

"Yes. I think so. I don't know."

"What's the matter with you, for God's sake!" His father sounded as if he were ready to cry. He had no right to do this to his father. Drugs would never have become a part of his life if Ray hadn't—

"I'll be all right," he told his father. "Can you meet me?"

There was silence on the other end. Finally, his father's voice came to him again. "I knew it would lead to this some day. I knew it, Ray. I should have had you put away. I should have called the cops in the very beginning. I should—"

"Jesus Christ, am I going to get another sermon?" Ray flared. He bit his tongue quickly, lowered his voice. "I'm—I'm sorry, Dad. I shouldn't have—I'm sorry. But I'm in trouble. Bad trouble."

"I understand," his father said. "Where do you want me to meet you?"

"There's a place on The Street—Fifty-second Street—it's called Conlee's. Between Fifth and Sixth. You can't miss it. Meet me there."

"What time?"

"What time is it now?"

"Twelve-thirty."

"Give me half an hour."

"All right."

"Dad? You'll—you'll bring some money? Ten bucks?"

"Yes."

"Thanks. Thanks."

He replaced the receiver rapidly, looked once more at the dead Eileen Chalmers, her face white against its halo of hair. He shivered in a new muscular spasm, then opened the door and left the room quietly.

Half an hour is a long time to wait—especially when you're overdue. He was overdue. Brother, was he overdue! His stomach seemed to be wrapped around his spine. He couldn't keep his hands still, even though he'd jabbed them deep into his pockets. He kept shivering, and he looked at the people who passed, wondering if they knew he was an addict.

How does a guy get this way, he asked himself?

The other question followed immediately, the way it always did. How does a guy *stop* being this way?

You just stop, they all told him. How many times had his father sung that same tune? *Look, Ray, be sensible. This thing is all in your mind. Once you set your mind against it, you've got it licked.* Sure, sure, they all knew.

Ask an addict, though. Ask an addict how to get off the merry-go-round. See what he told you. All in the mind, sure. His father should be inside his stomach now. His father should see how much "mind" was involved. Where the hell was he? What was keeping him?

The merry-go-round is an easy thing to hop onto. It goes slowly at first, so that you can walk around with it and jump on whenever you feel like it. Later, when it starts spinning crazily, you can't jump off; you just can't. You keep reaching for the gold ring, but you never quite get it.

How had he started? On a job, he guessed. That was when he'd smoked his first joint. A pang of remorse whispered up into his throat, and he withdrew his hands from his pockets, watched them tremble violently.

Had he once played the piano? It seemed impossible. They should cut a record of him now. It'd be the greatest thing ever heard.

The first joint, a stick of marijuana, a harmless thing that made him feel just a little giddy, made him laugh a little too loudly. That was all. Nothing to it, really. No great kicks, nothing really.

The second stick was a little different. He knew what to expect this time, and this time the smoke seemed to whirl into his mind, sweeping away all the cloudiness, all the cobwebs, and everything was crystal-clear, as glowing as a diamond, as sharp as the glistening edge of a dagger. He'd swung that second time, really swung, and he went on swinging for half the night, feeling so damned good. He was as sharp as a tack, and he knew so much. He could sit there smugly and watch the poor fools prancing around. He could sit there with a tight little smile on his lips, and a secret enjoyment inside him, with his mind functioning like a well-tuned machine.

He liked it then. He went back to it. It wasn't expensive, and he enjoyed the feeling.

And then somebody gave him a sniff of the big stuff. He'd dreamt he was swimming under water the first time. And the fish moved silently around him, swishing, swishing. And there were brilliant coral fans and luminescent eyes, and the warm gentle lap of the water.

That had been cocaine. He had continued snorting it until someone told him the drug would destroy the mucus membranes in his nose. He had seen graphic enough proof, had seen snorters with open sores on their nostrils. He had learned, too, that heroin was easier to get than cocaine. Most addicts were on H, and the demand dictated the supply, and so he had made a heroin buy, and someone had shown him how to cook the deck, how to shoot it into his arm. He had started with simple skin pops until someone else told him that mainlining was the only way.

From the first snort to the first mainline shot there had been a total of exactly two months. At the end of that time, he was hooked—and unlike most addicts, he was willing to admit he was hooked, even though such an admission was made with revulsion and reluctance. He had hopped on an innocent-looking merry-go-round, and suddenly the carrousel had begun to pick up speed. It was at top speed now, and it would never slow down, never. He needed a shot every four hours, like clockwork, right on the button. Keep that shot from him and his entire system began to scream for it.

Where did the merry-go-round end? Did it ever run down?

Maybe it had run down already.

Maybe it had run down with the body of a blonde singer stretched out on a hotel bed with two slugs in her belly. Maybe—

"Ray!" The voice was soft, with an undertone of anxiety in it. He turned rapidly, took his father by the arms.

"Dad, Jesus, what kept you?"

"Let's go inside," his father said.

"Sure, sure." He held open the door, his lips moving nervously, his teeth rattling. "Did you bring the money, Dad?"

"Yes, I brought it."

"Good, good." He laughed a quick, forced laugh. "Good."

They walked inside, past the bar with the lights streaming through the lined-up bottles, past the phone booths, into the rear of the place, a dimly lit rectangle surrounded by a dozen or so round tables.

"Sit down, Dad, sit down," he offered, pulling a chair out.

He hated himself while he went through the buttering-up routine, but he went through it. He had no choice, he told himself. He had to have money, and he was going to get it.

They sat down together, and he leaned across the table, staring into his father's face.

"How—how much did you bring?"

"Tell me about the dead girl," his father said. He was a small man with an aquiline nose and soft brown eyes. The eyes were moist and deep now, spaniel-like, and Ray felt again the deep guilt for having complicated his father's simple, easy life. His father—

"The girl?" Ray snapped himself back to the scene in the hotel room. "She's dead, Dad. I left her in the room."

"How much did you steal from her?"

"*What?*"

"I said—"

"I heard you! I heard you, all right." Sudden indignation flooded over Ray. "Are you crazy or something?"

"I knew it would come to this, Ray."

"You don't know what you're talking about." His hands were trembling again, more violently this time. He tried to calm himself. He couldn't blame his father for jumping to conclusions. "I know what, you're thinking, Dad, but it isn't the goods. Look, look, I haven't got time to talk. I—I need a shot. I need it real bad."

"Is that why you wanted the money?"

"Yes."

Ray watched his father's face, and he knew something of the struggle that was going on within the older man.

"I can't give you money for that stuff, Ray. I can't. I'd feel like a murderer."

"I know, Dad, I know. You're right, Dad. But this is different. I need the stuff. I've got to figure this out. I need a little time to think straight."

"What do you have to figure out?" Mr. Stone asked.

"This whole business, this thing. The girl, I mean. She's dead, don't you understand?"

"Ray," Mr. Stone asked quietly, "why didn't you go to Lexington when I asked you to?"

Ray felt his patience beginning to snap. He needed a shot, that's all, a shot, a lousy shot, and he had to go through all this crap. What did he have to do, get down on his knees? Why couldn't they understand that he had to have it, that his body was screaming for it, that if he didn't get it soon he'd rip the goddam table in half with his bare hands? Jesus. *Jesus!*

"I didn't want to go to Lexington. I'm no damned criminal. I've heard all about Lexington, thank you."

"From whom? From your fellow dope f—"

"Don't say it! Don't say it," Ray shouted. That was it, that was the breaking point. He was through kidding. "You've been reading too many comic-book exposés," he said angrily.

"This could all have been avoided," Mr. Stone said.

"Sure. But it wasn't. It wasn't, you see." He began to tap his heels on the floor. "I need a shot. I need money. I have to have a shot." He was beginning to speak curiously, his words tumbling out one after the other, He knew this, and he was powerless to stop it. He didn't care anyway. He didn't care how he sounded. He wanted that money.

He couldn't sit any longer. He stood up abruptly, began pacing back and forth before the table, clenching and un-clenching his fists.

"Are you going to give me the money, or do I get it else-where?" he demanded.

Mr. Stone reached out and put his hand on Ray's arm. "Sit down, son. No need to get excited."

Ray remained standing, hating what he knew was coming, but making no attempt to stop his voice. "Do I get the money? I have to get out of here or I'll bust wide open. I have to get that shot, can you understand? I can't hang around here if you're not giving me any money."

"I'll give you the money, son. Sit down."

He reached for his wallet, and Ray sat clown, sighing deeply. "I'm sorry, Dad. Really, I'm sorry." He cradled his head in his hands. "Why do I always have to beg you? Why can't you understand what it's like?" He looked across at his father.

"You're going to be all right, son," Mr. Stone said. Ray saw his father's eyes shift imperceptibly to the bar, then back to the wallet he'd placed on the table. Immediately, Ray's eyes leaped to the mirror over the bar. Two blue-uniformed figures were reflected in that mirror.

Ray's mouth fell open, and he turned accusing eyes on his father.

"I called them," Mr. Stone said, a peculiar sadness around his mouth. "They'll cure you, Ray."

Ray pushed his chair back quickly, darting a hasty glance at the figures in the mirror again.

"Cure me? With what? The electric chair?"

He looked again at the mirror, saw one of the cops draw his revolver. Quickly, he snatched the wallet off the table, stuffed it into his jacket, and ran to the piano standing against the back wall. Silently, he thanked his memory, thanked the fact that he'd chosen a place he knew well. Without hesitation, he pitted his shoulder against the piano, felt the muscles tighten as he heaved. The piano rolled away, revealing an exit door bolted with a huge two-by-four on metal brackets. He lifted the lumber, dropped it heavily to the floor.

"Ray!" his father called. "Come back! They'll help you!"

"I don't need their help," Ray shouted as he threw open the door. The bright sunlight hurt his eyes for a moment, and he shielded them with his hand. He looked into the room once more, saw one of the cops raise his gun, heard the blast as the cop fired over his head into the ceiling.

He ran out into the alley, heard the tear of another slug whipping into the door jamb. His nerves were tangled into a vibrating crisscross, and his stomach ached, and his muscles shook with blunt pain. But he ran.

He ran like a dazed rabbit, out of the alley and onto the sidewalk. He looked rapidly to his right, his left, then sprinted toward Fifth Avenue, smashing into a woman in a mink coat, almost knocking her down, untangling himself from the leash with the poodle on its end, and then breaking into a run again.

He ran, and the sun slanted down crazily, reflecting in the windows he passed, dancing back into his eyes with blazing intensity. He passed faces, faces, heard the hoarse shouts behind him, the sharp crack of a revolver followed immediately by another blast from a second gun.

He reached Fifth, turned the corner rapidly, ran into the crowd, stumbling, pushing, faster, faster. His lungs burned and his eyes smarted, and he needed a shot more than anything in this great, wide, sweet world, but he kept running.

He passed the perfume shops, the luggage stores, turned into Rockefeller Plaza, ran past the flower beds, past the diners on the pavilion, past the United Nations flags fluttering in the breeze, out into the street again. What street was it? Where was he?

He didn't care. He ran, dodging cars, jumping at the sudden blast of horns, knocking people aside.

He was in the arcade under the Hotel Roosevelt, running, running, his shoes clacking against the floor of the long corridor. He pushed through the revolving doors at the end of the corridor, ran past the pay lockers and the phone booths, turned to his right and ran into a small waiting room, a part of Grand Central Station.

He stopped running just inside the door, looked around him hastily, and then slowly walked toward a bench. He sat down, his breath coming in painful gasps. Slowly, almost afraid of what he'd see, he looked back over his shoulder toward the doors.

He'd lost the cops.

He released his breath in a thankful sigh, and listened to the announcements of the incoming trains.

## Chapter Three

He sat for three anxious minutes, watching the big clock on the wall. He looked at the doors again, then turned his eyes back to the clock and painfully counted off another three minutes. Quickly, he turned to the doors again, relieved when he saw the stream of people in civilian clothes pushing their way through into the waiting room. No police. Good.

He reached into his hip pocket and took out his father's wallet, rapidly sliding open the zipper. His fingers groped into the bill compartment, reaching hungrily.

One, two...

His fingers froze. He spread the bills apart, a frown crossing his forehcad. Maybe some bills were stuck together, maybe they were new bills.

No, there were just two of them. Just two lousy singles. But he'd said he'd bring ten; he'd promised. Maybe he kept his money scattered. Maybe he was one of those people who are always prepared for holdups.

Quickly, he unsnapped the coin compartment, dug into it with two fingers, found nothing. He thumbed through the snapshots in the wallet, sticking his fingers down into the celluloid cases. Nothing. Nothing, *nothing!*

He looked up suddenly as he realized how strange his behavior must seem. He stuffed the wallet back into his pocket, holding the two crumpled bills in his hands.

What could he do with two dollars? Two dollars would never buy a full deck, and in his condition nothing less than a full deck would set him straight. Two bucks. He cursed his father, then shook his head tiredly as he realized his father had only been trying to help him. He glanced down at the singles again, marveling at the way his hands shook.

Maybe Louie would give him a break. Maybe if he explained it all to Louie, he'd give him a break. He grinned for the first time that day, amazed that he could find anything funny in his present position. My keeper, he thought. Louie, good old Louie. A slimy bastard, oh yes, a very slimy bastard, a louse—but he holds the key. In another time, Ray Stone would have crossed the street just to avoid the sight of Louie. But now, ah now, how the mighty hath fallen. Ray Stone, one-time piano player, all-around good mixer, and nice fellow. *Now*, maybe Louie would give him a break. Maybe scurvy Louie with his rotten teeth and his foul breath, maybe Louie out of the goodness of his kind heart would allow Ray Stone to shoot a deck of horse into his arm for the price of two bucks. Maybe.

It was worth a try. He got up rapidly, walked out of the waiting room, stopped at one of the cigar stands, and changed a single. He walked past the knot of service men standing near the phone booths across from the cigar stand, and picked the booth farthest in. Rapidly, he dialed the number.

It rang several times. He drummed his fingers against the metal of the booth, his knees jiggling nervously.

"Yeah?"

The voice almost surprised him. It was the familiar voice, the voice he hated, but the voice he'd come to know and need.

"Louie?"

"Yeah, who's this?"

"Ray."

"Who?"

"Ray Stone."

"Say, what's the idea calling me here?" Louie protested. "You anxious for trouble?"

Ray felt every nerve in his body tense as he prepared to apologize. "I'm—I'm sorry, Louie. I had to call." Crawl, Stone, he told himself. Crawl to the man with the key.

"All right, all right, what is it?"

Ray glanced through the glass door of the booth, uneasily eying the people outside.

"I need a fix."

Louie was silent for several seconds. "Where you calling from, Stone?"

"A booth in Grand—"

"Call me back from a private phone. I can't take—"

"Louie, just a second. I can't get to a private phone."

"All right, just make it fast. There's a meet at Lenox and one-three-five. Got that? Lenox and—"

"I've only got a deuce, Louie. Can you fix me for a deuce?"

"You know the price of a deck, Stone."

"Just this time, Louie. I'm—I'm in a bad way."

"The monkey's scratching, eh Stone? Too bad, but business is business. I can let you have only a cap for two bucks."

"Look, Louie, I'll give you the deuce and my cuff links. How's that? How's that, Louie?" He was crawling on his belly now, right down on the ground, his nose pressed to Louie's feet.

"N.G., Stone. Hock the links. I got all the jewelry I need."

"Louie, have a heart. The shops are closed. This is Sunday!"

"A cap for a deuce, Stone, and you're getting a bargain. A deck is five, you know that."

"Give me a deck for the deuce, Louie. I'll pay you tomorrow. As soon as I can get—"

"Sure, sure, everybody'll pay me tomorrow. *Mañana* never comes, Stone. A cap, take it or leave it."

Ray's temper snapped then, and he was suddenly tired of kissing Louie's backside. "Look, you little—"

"So long, Stone."

"Louie—"

There was a dull click, and Ray stared at the receiver, dazed.

"He hung up," Ray said aloud. "That lousy son of a bitch! He hung up!"

Ray slammed the receiver down onto the hook, clenching his fist into a tight ball. He felt insane frustration boil up inside him, felt his reason flood from his body. He skinned back his lips, and his eyes blazed. Furiously, he smashed his fist against the side of the booth, feeling the metal bite into his knuckles. He drew the fist back quickly, and threw it at the metal again, blood spurting on his skinned knuckles. He sat breathing heavily for a few seconds, working his mouth noiselessly. Then he threw open the door and pushed his way past the people waiting to use the phone, brushing them aside with his wide shoulders. He was beginning to tremble again. And he was beginning to feel sick.

It was going to get worse, a lot worse, a hell of a lot worse, unless he did something about it real soon. Again he wondered how he could have left himself so wide open. You'd think after all these months he'd know better, know enough to have a spare shot ready all the time, especially in the morning. He really couldn't be blamed for this one, though. When he'd sacked in last night, he'd expected to wake up to sixteen ounces of the stuff.

Thinking of it made it worse. He wanted to tear something, hit something, knock down somebody, anybody, anything, anything to untangle him. But he knew the only thing that would set him straight.

All right, all right, you know, he told himself. But where are you going to get it?

I don't know, he moaned inwardly, the thought twisting his

mind. I don't know, and he felt the sickness at the pit of his stomach again.

Maybe Jeannie would— No, no, she wouldn't. But maybe. No, he couldn't. He, couldn't go to her again, he couldn't. He moistened his lips. Maybe she'd forgotten about the time he— Maybe she'd— No, it wasn't worth the trip. But he needed a shot.

His body was covered with sweat now, his shirt sticking to his back. He gulped, felt the lump rise and fall in his throat. Maybe Jeannie would give him some money. Maybe, just maybe, just maybe one chance in a hundred million, maybe, maybe.

He made up his mind quickly, walked up the ramp to the street and hailed a taxicab, gambling with his last dollar and ninety cents.

The cab ride made him sicker, and he was glad when it was over. He paid the cabbie, pocketing the remaining seventy-five cents. He looked up at the third-floor window, then rapidly climbed the front steps and opened the glass-framed door. He pushed Jeannie's bell, nervously wetting his lips, waiting for the buzz that would open the inside door. He pressed the bell again, still waiting, his fingers moving restlessly on the knob. Disgusted, he pushed all the bells in the small entranceway, quickly opened the door as a chorus of buzzes sounded.

He ran up the steps to the third floor, stopping outside 3B. He leaned on the buzzer, hearing it sound deep within the apartment. What time was it? Was she still sleeping? Come on. Come on!

Inside, he heard a restless stirring. "All right," a voice called. "Just a minute." He released the button and waited while he heard footsteps coming toward the door. The door opened a crack and he stuck his foot into the wedge. A blue eye appeared in the crack, then widened in surprise. "Ray!"

"Open up, Jeannie," he said.

He saw her shake her head, only part of her features visible in the slit of the door. "No, Ray. Please go away."

"I want to come in, Jeannie."

"You're—you're not welcome here, Ray. Go away. Please."

"I need help," he said, keeping his foot stuck in the wedge.

He saw her brush a strand of auburn hair out of her eyes, remembered the gesture from somewhere deep in his memory, felt a momentary pang of nostalgia. "I thought you didn't want help anymore, Ray. I thought—"

"I need a fix," he said desperately.

"You've come to the wrong place, Ray."

"I need money." His teeth were on edge now, and he hoped she wouldn't give him trouble. All she had to do was slip him a fin, just slip it through the crack. She didn't have to let him in if she didn't want to. All she had to do was slide it through that opening. That's all he wanted.

"I haven't any money, Ray."

His face began to twitch, the muscles around his lips, the muscles near his eyes. His whole face twitched as if it would fall apart, leaving only a skull. He saw the panic in her eyes, saw her grip her lower lip between her teeth, saw the tears almost start.

"Jeannie," he said softly, "please let me in. We'll sit down and talk this over. Please, Jeannie."

"We've said all there is to say, Ray. Please, please, leave me alone, please."

"No!" he shouted, and he heaved his shoulder against the door, slamming it into her body. He felt a faint resistance, and then a yielding as he pushed into the room. He slammed the door behind him.

Jeannie sat on the floor, her legs folded under her, her skirt twisted. He stared down at her. He brushed his hand across his eyes, trying to forget that this was Jeannie, his Jeannie. He shook his head abstractly, wiped the sweat from his upper lip. "Jeannie—"

She pulled her skirt over her knees, then buried her face in her hands. Her shoulders heaved as she began sobbing.

"Jeannie—"

"Take what you want and go," she said. "Please. Just go. Just go— Just—"

He dropped to his knees and put his arm around her shoulders, remembering the way it used to be. His girl, Ray Stone's girl. Standing by the piano with the smile in her eyes and on her lips, and that look on her face that said he was her man, good or bad. He blinked his eyes. There was a burning sensation in his throat. That was long ago. How long ago? He couldn't remember. He felt so old, old at twenty-six, a lifetime lived at twenty-six. And Jeannie was crying again. He'd made her cry again, just like before. He was always hurting people now. That's all he was good for.

He patted her shoulder awkwardly, then jumped to his feet. He needed money. She could cry with tears, but she didn't know how he was crying inside. Every cell, every tissue, every nerve, every fiber, every muscle was crying inside him.

He walked hastily to the bedroom in the familiar apartment. He found her purse on the dresser, opened it and took out two fives and a single, his fingers shaking as he pocketed the bills. How many times had he stolen in the past year? How low can you get, how dirty rotten low…

Eleven dollars! More than enough. Enough for two decks, with some left over. Two great big decks. His lips shook and he clamped his teeth tightly together, but they still shook.

Quickly, he walked back into the foyer. She was still on the floor, bent over now, her head cradled in her arms, her hair spilling over onto the carpet.

"I'm sorry, Jeannie," he said. "But—" He gulped hard. "You know—"

She looked up. Her eyes found his, silently pleading.

She stared at the money in his hand, begging him with her eyes to put it back. He looked down at the bills, suddenly remembered what they would buy and opened the door.

"You're better off this way, Jeannie," he said. "You're better off without me."

He watched her head nod and then shake, nod and shake. She kept sobbing, her shoulders trembling. He couldn't watch anymore. He closed the door behind him and ran down the steps.

He had the money now. He would call Louie, call the man with the key. He would tell the little bastard he had the money, ram it down his throat, shove it all the way down. He had the money.

Louie had said the meet was on 135th and Lenox. He wondered what time it would be? He'd call Louie again and find out. But this time, he wouldn't crawl.

He stopped by the candy store on the corner, reaching for some change in his pocket. His eye caught the newspaper on the stand. It was an extra edition, probably dumped on the stands a few moments before.

The headline was big and black. POLICE SEEK ADDICT.

He recognized the picture under the headline. He recognized it because it was the one he'd taken when he graduated from high school.

He felt sick again, and he ran into the candy store.

## Chapter Four

The candy store owner had a thin, hatchet face. He wore glasses that reflected the rays of the sun, looking like two molten pools of gold on either side of his curving nose.

Ray looked into the glistening pools, and they shimmered and swam out of focus. He gripped the top of the marble counter, and his lips worked anxiously as he struggled for words.

"Bro—bromo. Gimm—"

He didn't know what he wanted. He wanted something. He had to have something to push against the churning waves that threatened to erupt in his stomach. Ray felt the nausea spring up inside him again. He knew what he needed now. It sure as hell wasn't a bromo.

"Bathroom!" he blurted, his hand going up to his mouth.

"Jesus!" the storekeeper said. He came out from behind the counter, his apron smeared with chocolate syrup. He took Ray's arm. "Jesus!" he said again. Quickly, he started walking Ray to the back of the store. Now, with his back to the sun, the storekeeper's glasses had turned transparent again, and Ray saw narrow brown eyes behind them. He looked into the eyes, and shame swept over his body, shame that he had to be led to the bathroom by a stranger.

"Right in there," the storekeeper said. He opened a door and practically shoved Ray inside. "Lift the seat," he cautioned.

Ray gripped the porcelain bowl and braced himself against the wave starting at the pit of his stomach. God, he was sick. Good God, he was sick. His eyes sprang water, and the tears ran down his cheeks as his body was turned inside out. The smell of waste flooded into his nostrils, mingled with the heavy odor of urine in the close room. Again the nausea swept over him and a new paroxysm seized his stomach. Again. Again.

And finally, he was hanging limply over the bowl, sweat mingled with the tears on his face. He pushed himself upright, his hand fumbling for the flush handle. The sound of the water roared in his ears as he staggered toward the small sink. He turned on the cold water, doused his face. He felt a little better. He stood upright, straightened his tie, let out an exhausted sigh. His eyes met their own reflection in the mirror. He stared at them, oblivious to the rest of his features. They were bright, almost feverish, a deep gray against the pallor of his face. Addict's eyes. Ray Stone, hophead.

Shut up, he screamed mentally, shut up, shut up! He was still breathing heavily. He swallowed deeply, trying to compose himself before he went out to meet the sober brown eyes of the storekeeper. At last he felt calm enough, and he stepped out of the tiny room, closing the door gently behind him. He walked to the counter, climbed up on a stool. He looked up at the storekeeper, wondering if he knew an addict was sitting on one of his stools.

"A glass of seltzer," he said. His eye caught the newspapers stacked on the counter. Quickly, he snatched one from the top of the pile, looked at his picture, and hastily turned to page three for the story.

The storekeeper set the glass of seltzer in front of Ray, a wet smear trailing behind it.

"Big head, eh?" he asked.

"Huh? Oh. Oh yes."

"I always stay away from it myself during the day." Ray nodded. There was a picture of Eileen Chalmers on the third page, a picture taken when she was still alive. She was smiling happily, standing next to a thin man who grinned self-consciously at the photographers. The text under the picture read: *Eileen Chalmers, lovely victim of West Side hotel slaying, about to embark on honeymoon with her bandleader husband, Dale Kramer, just after their marriage last April.*

"You young fellows," the storekeeper said. "Cast-iron stomachs, that's what you've got. It catches up with you, though. Got to be careful."

Ray nodded again, his eyes scanning the story. *Police are hunting the city for Raymond Stone, believed to be a drug addict…last seen with the dead girl…Hotel Stockmere…clerk described Stone as being tall, well-built, with blond hair… believed by police that Stone will be apprehended shortly… need for drug will lead him to seek contacts for securing…*

"Hey, you ain't touched your seltzer," the storekeeper said.

"What?" He looked up into the inquiring brown eyes. "The seltzer, yes, thank you." He lifted the glass, sipped a little of it, his eyes running down to where he'd left off on the page.

*…contacts for securing…*They had it sewed up tight! *Albert Stone, father of the suspect, expressed the desire that his son be captured…help him, he believed…cure him…*

Futility flooded over Ray, a hopeless wash of futility that left him weak. He felt tears behind his eyes, quickly ducked his head to read the rest of the story.

*Dale Kramer, currently appearing at the Trade Winds, made no comment on the brutal shooting of his wife…Miss Chalmers was twenty-two years old, a singer with—*

Rapidly, he closed the newspaper, stared at his picture on the front page. He realized the man behind the counter was staring at the picture, too. He folded the paper, tucked it under his arm.

"How much?"

The storekeeper eyed him quizzically, his eyes narrowing. "Two cents for the seltzer, five for the paper." He grinned. "Should really charge you for use of the can."

Ray didn't smile back. Stacked on the counter, facing the storekeeper, was the pile of newspapers. Quickly, Ray dug into his pocket, put down a nickel and two pennies. He was beginning to tremble again. At first he thought it was fear, the fear of having his picture splashed across the front page, and the fear of those little brown eyes across the counter studying his face. But he recognized it for what it really was almost instantly.

He still needed a shot.

He started walking out of the candy store, and the storekeeper walked down to the end of the counter, standing just in front of the stacked newspapers now.

*Run!* something screamed inside Ray's head. *Run, run!*

He reached the sidewalk, afraid to look back, afraid to show his face to those scrutinizing eyes behind their magnifying lenses again. He turned to his left, started walking to the corner.

"Hey!" the storekeeper's voice came to him. "Hey! Hey, you, stop!"

The voice exploded inside his head, sending skyrockets of warning to every nerve in his body. He started running instantly, dropping the newspaper, turning at the corner and barreling up the street. Behind him he heard the storekeeper shouting, "Stop that man! That's the addict!"

Addict, addict, addict. His feet pounded against the pavement, his eyes searching the street for a cab. Addict. They'd labeled him, tagged him, tied him up with a pretty yellow ribbon.

They'd tagged him, all right, every single one of them. They'd all be looking for the dope fiend, the man who put two slugs into a pretty blonde's belly. Except he wasn't that man.

And except one other thing. It wasn't *they* who had tagged him; he'd tagged himself. He'd tagged himself the moment he hopped on the merry-go-round.

A yellow cab loomed large alongside the curb. He yanked open the door, piled into the back seat. "Uptown," he said, still panting. "Just drive." The cabbie flicked down his flag, threw the vehicle into gear and stepped on the gas. Ray lurched back against the leather seat, his thoughts running wildly through his mind.

First he needed a shot. He had to get that shot first, then everything else would take care of itself. But how? Good God, how was he going to get a shot? The police knew he was an addict. They'd be watching all the pushers, Louie included. Maybe he could sneak past them, get to Louie somehow.

The eleven dollars in his pocket seemed to grow, expand, seemed ready to burst out of his trousers. Eleven bucks, and no way to get a fix. Eleven bucks, his mind tormented him, two decks' worth, two sweet beautiful decks of horse, eleven dollars sweating in his pocket, and the monkey scratching away at his back, getting heavier now, getting real heavy, getting too heavy for a man to carry. How much could he take? How long would it be before he was sick again?

The buildings outside flashed by in gray-brown blurs, and he thought of the city, of the immensity of it, of a fourteen-year-old kid fumbling with the intricate fingering of "Rhapsody in Blue," a kid named Ray Stone.

"Doesn't Raymond play beautifully?" his mother used to say. He could still remember her, a tall blonde woman, regal in her stature. Her friends spoke quietly and distinctly and balanced teacups and cake plates on their knees.

And in contrast, he could remember the simple comforts his father desired, the uncomplicated structure of a family life without the pomp and ceremony of countless friends at countless afternoon teas or cocktail parties or late-morning brunches.

His mother liked people, liked to be surrounded with them. His father did not. It was as simple as all that and, conversely, as complicated as all that. It added up to what the marriage counselors called incompatibility. He supposed the eventual breakup was evident even when he was younger than fourteen. He did not become fully aware of the constant friction until then, though, and he marveled that the marriage actually lasted another two years.

They separated when Ray was sixteen. His mother went to Reno for the divorce, the way other people in her circle of friends had done. Ray spent six months out of every year with his mother and six months with his father. He fully understood what had happened, but understanding in no way lessened the burden of grief he carried.

He attacked the piano with a new determination. He would really play, would really learn to play. And when his mother said, "Doesn't Raymond play beautifully?" it irritated the hell out of him because he wasn't playing to satisfy her but to satisfy a new need within him. And when his father said, "Your piano's really coming along, son," it irritated him as much because he knew he was coming along well, but he felt he wasn't coming along fast enough. The city in those days became a warm romantic place to him. Somehow, he had been denied love in a loveless marriage, and he sought it everywhere around him, and found it hidden in the corners of the city. He had spun the city's melody on his keyboard, felt its bigness in his fingers and his heart.

And then people began noticing when Ray Stone played, just like the corny bits in Hollywood musical comedies, where the janitor stops sweeping to listen when the new star performs, just like that, except that the men who were listening weren't sweepers. They were musicians, and good musicians, and they recognized promise in Ray's talent—not achievement, because achievement was not yet there. He had been booked for jobs from the time he was eighteen. He had played every conceivable job offered. He had scooped them all up like a squirrel busily gathering nuts against the coming winter. He wanted his talent to grow, and he wanted experience, and so he accepted them all—the Irish weddings and the Italian weddings and the Jewish weddings, the club dates where there were big dance floors, or little dance floors, or no dance floors, the bar dates where he played piano for drunks, and the jobs outdoors on park malls; and once he borrowed an accordion and played in a marching band, anything and everything to keep his talent growing. He had met Jeannie on a job, and he had also met narcotics on a job, and that was when the promise had withered and died.

He had once loved the city because the city was warm, and the city had helped him nurture his talent. But now the city was a place in which to hide, a place in which to plot, a place in which to seek out a pusher. Twelve years, that was all. So much had happened to the kid with the dreaming fingers. He was twenty-six now, and his talent, his promise, what had happened to—

"Any place in particular, Mac?" the cabbie asked.

Ray looked up and glanced through the window, trying to get his bearings. "On the corner," he said. "That'll be fine."

The cab ground to a stop and Ray opened the door. He gave the cabbie a dollar, told him to keep the change, leaving himself ten dollars and a little more, just enough for the two decks.

Yes, he would have to get past the police, find Louie somehow. Another call should do the trick. What was Louie's number again? He probed his memory. If only he could think straight, if only everything weren't jumping up and down inside him. He started to think of the syringe, of the sting of the needle in his arm, the spreading warmth, the numbing sensation. He began to sweat. Yes, yes, he'd have to get that shot soon or go crazy, go babbling down the street like a madman.

His picture in the paper. He'd have to do something about that. Blond hair was a dead giveaway—thank you, Mother, for your powerful genes. His eye caught a big shoe swinging in the breeze over a shop. Across the side of the shoe, in red letters, was the word "Repairs." He walked to the glass-paneled door and opened it. A heavy man with a handlebar mustache looked up as Ray closed the door behind him.

"I want some black shoe polish," Ray said. "The liquid stuff. In a bottle, you know."

The shoemaker got him what he wanted without a word. Ray paid him and left.

On West Sixty-third Street he found a small hotel, registered under the name of Ralph Surrey, and then went to work on his hair. He thought fleetingly of the two bucks the room was costing him, two bucks that took a sizable chunk out of the second deck he'd planned for. Maybe one deck would hold him until to-morrow, though. Then he could hock his links and maybe even his jacket. As always, when he thought of the drug, an excitement shivered up his spine. He tried to hold his hands steady as he stood over the sink in the bathroom and poured the black liquid into the bowl. As the liquid rose against the white porcelain, he reached down for the stopper, making sure it was in tight. He dipped both hands into the thick polish then and began, working it into his hair.

It was sloppy going, but he was getting results. He looked at the strange face in the mirror, marveling at what a change the color of hair can make. Carefully, with all the patience of a beautician, he dug down deep, close to his scalp, making sure each blond strand was now black.

Finally, he surveyed himself in the mirror, pleased with his handiwork, convinced that he looked different. He pulled out the stopper and let the remainder of the polish flow down the drain. Then he rinsed out the sink and washed his hands. He wet the end of a towel and carefully rubbed at the few streaks of black that had dripped down onto his forehead and cheekbones. He noticed his eyebrows, naked blond against the phony of his hair, and a new panic seized him.

He wanted to cry. He felt the way he had when he was a kid and he'd spent hours building a sand castle only to have a bigger kid knock it down. He stared at the eyebrows, and a complete hopelessness flooded his mind. For several moments, the problem seemed insurmountable. His eyes looked down at the sparkling whiteness of the sink. He swallowed heavily, looked at his own sad reflection in the mirror.

The need for immediate action sparked suddenly within him. He ran his fingers through his drying hair, pulled them away black. Quickly, he daubed at his eyebrows, spreading the smears of polish into the sparse hair. Again, his fingers went to his hair and back to his eyebrows, away, back, away, back. And at last he breathed deeply, his brows as black as the hair on his head. He wet the edge of the towel and wiped the excess polish off his forehead. He wondered what the clerk would think when he walked out.

Was he going to walk out? What was the next move?

An unreasoning anger took hold of him, and his mouth set in outraged righteousness. What the hell! *He* hadn't shot the girl. *He* hadn't killed her. But he was an addict, that was it. Give

the police a juicy addict to play with and they'd blame him for
every nickel ever stolen from a blind man's cup. Well this was
one goddam addict they weren't going to decorate with the
Purple Shaft. Some lousy bastard had put two slugs in Eileen
Chalmers's stomach, and that same lousy bastard was keeping
him away from Louie and the H he needed so desperately.

The answer seemed logical and simple to him: find that bastard. Find him, and the pressure would be off. The cops would
have a new sucker to toy with. And then Ray Stone could contact
Louie or any other damned pusher in the city.

He rolled down his sleeves, fastened his cuff links.

All right, he'd find the murderer.

He almost laughed out loud at this. Sherlock Stone Holmes,
hophead. How does a hophead go about finding a murderer in
a city like New York? In fact, how does anybody find anybody
in New York? He grinned at his own predicament, realizing it
wasn't at all funny.

And the old thought came back, the bittersweet thought, the
thought that quickened his blood and tightened his muscles:
how could he get another shot? And soon?

He put this out of his mind, convinced he could get all the
heroin he needed if he could clear himself. He had to shake the
monkey, and to do that he had to shake the cops. He remembered the newspaper clipping and the picture of Eileen with her
husband. Dale Kramer, a name familiar to Ray. Kramer had once
fronted a society outfit, sweet music with a *boop-boop-be-doop*
beat. Strictly crow material, with muted horns and groaning
saxes. He'd traded this in for a new combo when bop came into
fashion, and had managed to keep up with the better bands,
pulling in the kids all over the country on his personal-appearance
tours.

If Ray had some questions to ask, Dale Kramer would be a
good place to start.

Ray put on his jacket, locked his room, and buzzed for the elevator. When the car stopped at his floor, the elevator boy didn't seem to notice the changed color of his hair. The elevator stopped, and Ray walked across the lobby, avoiding the desk and heading straight for a phone booth.

He looked up the number of the Trade Winds, then rapidly dialed it. It was too early for Kramer to be at the club, but perhaps he could get his home number. At any rate, it wouldn't hurt to—

"Trade Winds, good afternoon."

"Hello—ah—I wonder if you could give me some information?"

"What kind of information, sir?"

Ray hesitated. In the background, he heard a trumpet reaching for a high note. He listened as saxes joined the blaring brass. Then the entire ensemble came to an abrupt stop.

"Hello?"

"Yes," Ray said. "I'm still here."

"What kind of information did you wish, sir?"

The band started again, in the middle of a number, and the trumpet hit the upper register, with the saxes joining in again. This time they kept playing.

"I was wondering if you could let me have Dale Kramer's home number?"

There was a discreet cough on the other end of the wire.

"I'm sorry, sir. We're not allowed—"

"That's all right. Thanks."

He replaced the phone on its hook. That had been a rehearsal, all right. He'd been to enough of them to know what they sounded like. That meant that Dale Kramer was now at the Trade Winds. Ray nodded, and stepped out of the booth.

A pain sliced into his stomach, ripped across his gut. God, oh God, holy mother of— He gripped the door of the booth, held tightly, while the wave of pain looped over and then subsided. The hell with Kramer, the hell with Eileen, the hell with every-body. He had to get a shot. He'd die; he'd drop dead right here on the floor if he didn't get one.

You can't get one, his mind mocked. The cops are looking for you, you stupid bastard.

He shook his head, wiped the sweat from his forehead.

Outside, he hailed a cab and told the driver to take him to the Trade Winds.

The sounds came to him as he stood at the bar, the old familiar rehearsal sounds. They came from behind a closed door at the other end of the room, and a bouncer sat in front of that door, his heavy legs straddling a chair. Ray downed his drink hastily, put his trembling hands into his pockets, and walked across the room.

He stopped directly in front of the bouncer. The man had a wide face with heavy black eyebrows and cauliflower ears. His nose had been broken more than once.

Ray tried to look bored as he reached into his back pocket for his wallet. He flipped it open to his driver's license, closed it again before the bouncer took a good look.

"Police," he said tonelessly. "Dale Kramer in there?"

The bouncer licked his lips, then wiped away the wetness with the back of his hand. "He ain't gonna like you, Mac."

"I'm not interested in his likes or dislikes," Ray said coldly, his heart hammering in his chest. "His wife was murdered. I want to ask him a few questions."

The bouncer swung his leg over the chair, stood up, his shoulders wide against the door. "You and every other cop in New York," he said. He reached behind him, twisted the door knob, flicked open the door with a hair-covered hand. "He's the short one in the blue jacket."

"Thanks," Ray said. He stepped through the door, started walking quickly toward the bandstand. It had been too easy, too easy. There'd been nothing to worry about at all. He hadn't even needed the fortifying drink, and he began to regret the money he had paid for it, money that could have gone toward another shot. He heard the door close behind him, glanced over his shoulder to make sure the gorilla was on the other side of it. He was.

The boys in the band were lounging around the room, and Dale Kramer was penciling some marks onto a music sheet when Ray came up to him.

"Mr. Kramer?"

Kramer looked up. He was thin-faced, with high, protruding cheekbones and arching eyebrows. His eyes were green, and they went well with his slightly curving, feminine nose. A pencil-line mustache was sketched in over his upper lip, and his mouth opened now in surprise.

"Yes?" His voice was wary. He put the pencil down on the sheet, ran his hand over his thinning, black hair.

"Police," Ray said, giving the word as much conviction as he could.

Kramer screwed up his face. "Aren't you boys working overtime? You're the third one today. First there was Monaghan, and then—I forget his name. Big beefy guy with red hair." He lifted his eyebrows inquiringly. "Know who I mean?"

"Sure," Ray lied. "I won't take up much of your time, Mr. Kramer."

"That's what the other two said." He stood up, put his foot on the seat of the chair, carefully preserving the crease in his gabardine slacks. He rested his arms on the raised knee, hunched slightly forward. "All right, fire away," he said.

"I understand your wife was a singer," Ray said, not knowing exactly where to start.

"That's right, Mr.— I'm sorry, I didn't get your name."

"David. Lieutenant David."

"Mmmm. Yes, my wife was a singer."

"How come she wasn't singing with your band?"

"You all ask the same questions, don't you? What do you do, compare notes afterward?"

Ray smiled. "Sometimes." This was going fine. He was doing all right. He was beginning to *feel* like a cop.

"My wife used to sing with the combo, Lieutenant. In fact, she was on the band until a few months ago."

"Oh?"

"That's right. She left to join the Scat Lewis combo. You know Scat Lewis?"

"I've heard of him," Ray said.

"My wife was singing with him up until her death. He's playing at the Ace High, if you'd like to check."

"Don't you have a singer?" Ray asked. His eyes traveled over the men in the room.

"Sure. Barbara Cole." Kramer grimaced. "It gets complicated about here. Babs used to sing with Scat Lewis. She and Eileen arranged the switch. I got Babs, and Scat got Eileen, and everybody was happy."

"I see." Ray found his mind beginning to wander. He clamped his jaws together. He knew he'd be thinking of a shot again, and he wanted to keep that off his mind. "How come your wife left the band? Isn't that a little odd?"

"Not at all. She wanted to sing with Scat, and Babs wanted to sing with us. As simple as all that."

"Where's your singer now?"

"Never rehearses with the band," Kramer said. "You familiar at all with music?"

"No," Ray lied.

"Well, she's a bop singer, strictly ad lib. We give her a background, and she plays with it, understand? It comes out different every time. She improvises, you see. It wouldn't pay to have her at rehearsals."

"I see." A muscular spasm twitched across Ray's face, and Kramer stared at him curiously.

His eyes narrowed suspiciously. "You've got a bad tic there, Lieutenant."

"Yes. Yes, I have." Ray attempted a smile, but it froze on his face. A new spasm contorted his jaw muscles, and he fought for control of his crumbling face.

"Had a tenor man with a tic like that once," Kramer said. His voice was conversational, but his eyes were narrow, two green slashes above his high cheekbones.

"That right?" Ray asked. The spasm had ended, but his hands were beginning to tremble.

"Yeah." Kramer paused, studied Ray's face. "You're young for a lieutenant, aren't you?"

"Well—"

"What'd you say your name was, Lieutenant?"

Ray was beginning to sweat. He felt the cold dampness seep into his clothes. He wanted to get. out of there. Fast. "Davis," he answered. "Lieutenant Da—"

Kramer was on his feet, his head reaching to Ray's shoulder. "I could have sworn you said David a minute ago."

"Davis," Ray repeated, his face a ghastly white. "I've got to go now. Thanks for your help." He turned, started for the door.

"Just a second," Kramer said.

The old tight knot reached into Ray's stomach. He quickened his steps. Behind him, he heard Kramer move forward a few paces, heard the hushed whispers of the musicians, a clarinet lazily sliding up a C scale.

"Bruno!" Kramer shouted.

Ray began to run. The door swung open as he reached for the knob, and the bouncer blocked the opening with his burly frame.

"Stop him, Bruno," Kramer bellowed.

Ray ducked his head, pitched his shoulder against Bruno's chest. The bouncer threw up his hands too late. Ray felt the solid smash of flesh against flesh, and then Bruno was stumbling backward, fighting for his balance. He lost his footing, tumbled heavily to the floor as Ray ran past.

Bruno cursed loudly, tried to scramble to his feet. Ray heard Kramer screeching, heard the bartender shout something as his feet took him to the exit door.

He was running again, running, running. And the pain was with him once more, the pain that knifed his insides, twisting, gouging. He reached the door, shoved aside some people entering the club, darted out to the sidewalk and continued to run.

## Chapter Five

He stopped running somewhere along Sixth Avenue. A clock in a barbershop told him it was ten minutes to five. He walked up a few doors, stopped in the entrance of an art supply shop, pretended to be looking at the window display while he caught his breath.

Ten minutes to five. Christ, when had the last fix been? He tried to count back over the hours, succeeded only in visualizing a full-bodied blonde with a tin of heroin in her hands.

He'd have to contact Louie. Cops or no cops, he couldn't go on like this any longer. Quickly, he walked to a United Cigar store on the corner, stepped into a phone booth, and dialed Louie's number.

He let the phone ring sixteen times, counting each ring patiently, before he finally gave up.

He replaced the phone on the hook, sat in the booth with his hands folded in his lap. Outside the doors of the booth, outside the store, lay the city, immense and quiet in its Sunday austerity.

Out there is the bastard, he thought. Somewhere out there.

A consuming hatred flashed within him, and he knew he could easily strangle the son of a bitch if he got his hands on him. But how? How do you find a murderer?

He thought of the Ace High. Perhaps he could pick up a lead there. Or was the chance worth taking? How long would it be before Dale Kramer told the cops about the hair dye? And how soon after that would a new description of him be flashed?

He was alone, alone against the city, alone against the cops, alone against the guy who'd torn open Eileen Chalmers's stomach. That was the worst part, the being alone.

Sure, feel sorry for yourself, you stupid bastard. Whose fault is it but your own? I know, he answered mentally. But—

He caught himself abruptly. He was going psycho, having arguments with himself. He'd be talking out loud next, like a man with two heads in a heated debate.

All right, what now? Back to the room, or over to the Ace High? He made the decision quickly, and stepped out of the booth. What the hell, he had nothing to lose, really—except his life.

The Ace High was a carbon copy of every other club on the street. He glanced briefly at the small dance floor, the band-stand, the scattering of tables. Then he walked directly to the bar, climbing up on a stool next to a brunette. The girl had her back to him, and she didn't turn when he sat down. Ray signaled for the bartender.

"Yes, sir?" He was apple-cheeked with a shock of red hair that toppled over his wide forehead.

"Police," Ray said. The old fear nudged him again. He looked hard at the bartender's face, wondering if this was the same man who'd served him the night he met Eileen.

"This place is beginning to look like the Fifth Precinct," the bartender said. "Eileen Chalmers again?"

"That's right."

"Well, go ahead," the bartender said, shrugging his massive shoulders. "I can't understand it, though. I figured you guys had it all sewed up."

"Sewed up?"

"Sure. The hophead. He's your man, all right."

"Maybe not," Ray said.

"Well, you know your own business, I guess. But I've seen lots of junkies, and I wouldn't trust any of them as far as I can throw the Empire State Build—"

"We like to consider all the angles," Ray interrupted. He buried his face in his hands, the hot rage at being condemned simply because he was an addict flooding over him again.

"Tired, huh?" the bartender asked.

Ray pulled his hands away from his face. "Yes. Yes, I—"

"You don't have to explain. I can imagine what a chase the junkie is leading you guys."

"About Eileen Chalmers—" Ray started.

"Didn't have an enemy in the world," the bartender said. "Sweetest kid you'd want to know."

"Excuse me," a soft voice broke in.

Ray turned to face the warmest pair of brown eyes he'd ever seen. The girl next to him had swung around on her stool and was facing him now, her lips slightly parted, a Martini glass in one hand.

"I didn't mean to eavesdrop, but—" She shrugged one rounded, white shoulder expressively. Ray's eyes fled to the pulse beating in the hollow of her throat. She wore a low-cut green faille dress. Her legs were crossed, the green faille molding her hips and thighs tightly, her knees sleek in their nylons.

"That's all right," he said.

"I knew her quite well. Eileen, I mean." Her face looked apologetic. She wore her black hair short, hugging the sides of her face, a stray ebony wisp curling beneath one ear. An eyebrow was cocked against her forehead. Her nose was straight, her eyes heavily fringed. He stared at their incredible warmth.

"My name is Barbara Cole," she said. "I sing with Dale Kramer. He's her—"

"Yes, I know. Her husband."

In the background, Ray heard a nickel click in the juke, heard the swish of the arm, the record dropping. There was the faint murmur of brushes against a snare, the subtle thrum of a piano, and then the soaring sweep of a full sax section.

The girl lifted her glass and sipped slowly. She stared at Ray over the edge, leaned forward slightly. A muted trumpet joined the sax section, and she jiggled her foot in time with the music.

"Nice," she said.

"Yes."

"Are policemen allowed to dance on duty?" she asked. Her eyes met Ray's with open frankness.

"Well—"

She swung her legs around, reached for the floor with one foot. The dress slid up over her knee as she rose. "I think they are," she said.

She took his hand, and he climbed down from the stool. When they reached the postage-stamp dance floor, the record stopped. Ray turned his head, saw a short, fat man put another nickel in the machine. The music started again, and he took her in his arms. She was warm; warm and alive. He held the small of her back with his right hand, and he could feel the flesh beneath her dress.

She moved closer, pressing tight against him. He felt the swell of her breasts against him, the solidity of her thighs, the length of her legs close to his.

Her mouth was below his ear, and when she spoke, her voice rushed against his neck in breathless spurts.

"I arranged for Eileen to come on the Scat Lewis combo," she said.

"Really?"

"Yes. We sort of switched places."

"I see."

Her fingers were widespread on the back of his neck, and they began to move idly now.

"You dance nicely, policeman."

"Thank you."

She pressed closer to him. They danced silently for a few moments, and then she whispered, "I know a better dance floor."

He didn't answer. He listened to the music, and he smelled her hair, and he thought of Eileen. He thought of Eileen and the tin of heroin, and a new spasm of longing for the drug zigzagged through his body.

"Let's get out of here, policeman," she whispered.

The better dance floor turned out to be Barbara Cole's apartment in the Lower Eighties on Park Avenue.

It was expensive, all right. He could tell that at a glance. The floor was covered with a thick rug that made him want to take off his shoes and stretch his toes. A handsome sectional sofa faced a bar. A quick look at the labels on the bottles substantiated the money-smell about the whole place. Ray idly wondered who was paying for this elaborate shack.

"Not much," the girl said, "but it's home." She smiled at Ray, took off her short fur jacket and flipped it over the arm of an easy chair. "Like it?" she asked.

"Very nice, Miss Cole."

"I think we can stop that right now," she said, pouting prettily.

"Barbara?" he asked, testing the name.

"Babs will do fine, thank you."

"Babs then."

She walked to the bar. She began pouring whiskey into two water glasses.

"You're supposed to tell me yours now," she said, smiling back over her shoulder,

"Ray," he said quickly. His eyes widened as he realized what he'd done. Suppose she'd seen his name in the paper? He watched her curving back, hoping the name hadn't registered.

"Ray," she said, rolling it on her tongue, as if she were tasting fine wine. "What's the rest?"

"Ray Davis," he lied.

"Very nice. Here's a Scotch for Ray Davis."

She held out the glass and he took it eagerly. Maybe this was the ticket. Maybe he could get stinking drunk and forget the other pressing desire. Substitute one stimulant for another. He remembered how he used to smirk derisively at anyone who got high on alcohol. Alcohol, that was for meatballs.

"Let's drink to the hophead," she said.

He looked at her suspiciously. "Why him?"

"Why not? He probably needs a drink, wherever he is."

He needs a hell of a lot more than a drink, Ray thought.

"Sure," he said. "To the hophead."

They drank, and she put her glass down on the long coffee table in front of the sofa.

"Now, what can I do for you, policeman?"

"Well, what do you know about Eileen?" He sat on the sofa, and she sat down beside him.

"Nice kid," she said. "No morals, but nice."

"How do you know?"

"About her morals?" Babs smiled. "She's had a few men hanging around, and I assume she was a normal, red-blooded, American girl."

"With a normal, red-blooded, American husband."

"Dale never paid her much mind. I mean, he didn't like her fooling around, but he never did anything about it."

"He may have."

"How do you mean?"

"He may have killed her."

"I doubt it. Dale wouldn't touch a fly." She grinned, reached over for her glass.

"Who were these men in her life?" Ray asked.

Babs straightened, took a pull at her drink, sighed deeply. "Well, there's Charlie Massine. Ever hear of him?"

"No."

"She saw him just about every day. He's the drummer on Kramer's band. Pretty good, too."

"Was she—"

"Who knows? Knowing Charlie, I wouldn't doubt it for a moment."

"Who else?" Ray asked.

"Tony Sanders."

The name rang a familiar bell in his head. "The playboy?"

"The very same. He's been slumming with Eileen for quite some time now."

"And Kramer knew about all this?"

"Sure." She took another swallow. "And then there's Scat Lewis, a very nice guy. I wouldn't be surprised, though—"

"Your opinion of Eileen isn't a very high one, is it?"

"Don't get me wrong. I don't disapprove at all. I'm merely trying to give you a good picture of the situation." She paused and eyed Ray steadily. "After all, she wasn't a particularly discriminating person. The hophead who killed her—"

"We're not sure of that yet," he snapped.

"Well, at any rate, he was a pickup. And she had no scruples as far as he was concerned." She saw the look on his face and smiled. "You still don't understand, policeman. I'm not very moral, either."

He stood up. "Well—"

"Leaving so soon?" She rose with him, put one hand on his arm.

He thought of the pickup again, of Eileen's hotel room, of the heroin. He fought the desire that was climbing up into his throat, the need for the drug.

She moved close to him, leaning backward slightly.

"Let's dance some more, policeman."

"Why?" he asked.

Her eyes met his, held them in a solid grip. Her fingers tightened on his arms.

"Because I like the way you tremble when you dance."

"Trem—" He realized then that she'd mistaken his need for the drug as—

"Yes," she said softly. Her hands moved up behind his neck. "You tremble beautifully."

He found her lips against his, warm and moist. She dropped her hands to the small of his back, pulled him forward.

But he wasn't with it. He wasn't with it, and he knew he wouldn't be with it unless he could get a fix. Or unless he knew there would be a fix waiting when this was all over.

"Look," he said, moving his mouth away from hers. Her eyes had become smoky, and her heavy lashes almost touched now. She stared up at him in confusion. "This is no good," he said softly.

She tried to move close again, but he held her away. How many times, he wondered, had he left Jeannie while he'd gone in search of a needle? Poor kid, what he'd put her through.

He shook his head. "It's just no good," he said.

Her voice was husky when she answered. "I thought it was pretty damn good, myself."

"I mean—" he fumbled for an excuse. "I've got to be back at the station in ten minutes."

"Oh!" She smiled and moved up against him again. "For a minute there, I thought I was slipping."

She brought his mouth down against hers and her lips moved expertly. And then she pulled away, held him at arm's length, and looked up into his eyes.

"I just wanted to make sure you'd be back, policeman." She turned him around and started him for the door.

"Now go punch your clock."

# Chapter Six

Massine, Alfonso

Massine, Alfred

Massine, Bartholomew

Massine, Carol

Massine, *Charles*

He fumbled in his jacket pocket for a pencil, annoyed when he could find none. He glanced over toward the drug counter, saw that the clerk was busy, and hastily ripped the page from the phone book. He left the drugstore, paused outside to look at the address again. He folded the page and stuffed it into his side pocket. The large clock outside the jeweler's across the street said six-eighteen.

Ray knocked on the door and waited.

He was getting nervous again. He didn't like this kind of work. It made him sweat. And he didn't like the idea of being hunted. He'd passed three cops on the way to Charlie Massine's apartment, and each time his spine had curled up into his skull.

Impatiently, he knocked again.

"Hey, you want to break the door down?" The voice was deep and harsh. Ray took a deep breath as he heard heavy footsteps approaching the door. He steadied his hands by putting them into his pockets, then hastily withdrew them when the door began to open.

It opened wide, revealing a man almost as tall as Ray, with broad shoulders that tapered sharply to a narrow waist. He was wearing an undershirt and the curly black hair on his chest showed dark against the white of the cotton. He was clean-shaven, but there was a blue cast to his chin and cheeks. He eyed Ray with open distaste, studying his features.

"What college are you working your way through?" he asked. The irritated tone was still in his voice.

"I want to ask a few questions about Eileen Chalmers," Ray said.

Massine's face remained expressionless. "Yeah?"

"Yeah."

A flicker of recognition sparked in Massine's eyes. "Hey! You're the guy who broke up the rehearsal this after—"

Ray shoved his way into the room, slammed the door shut behind him. "That's right," he said. He was amazed by his own calmness. Maybe he'd licked the desire part. Maybe he wouldn't need it again for a while.

Massine walked over to a table, picked up a package of cigarettes. He speared one and hung it on his lower lip. Calmly, he lighted a match and held it to the tip.

"So now you're in," he said, blowing out smoke. "So now what?"

"What do you know about Eileen Chalmers?"

"Nothing."

Ray stepped closer to Massine. The drummer blew out more smoke. "Barbara Cole says you knew her."

Massine took a deep drag. "Oh sure, I knew her."

"Well, what about her?"

"I don't have to tell you nothing, bud. There's probably a million cops on your tail right now. All I have to do—"

Ray's voice was louder now. "Don't give me any crap, Massine. I'd break you in two before you picked up the phone. What do you know about Eileen?"

"You scare me, hophead."

"Don't get me sore, Massine."

The drummer recognized the threatening tone in Ray's voice. His hand paused on his cigarette, then he slowly removed it from his mouth. "I knew her on Kramer's band," he said. "She was Kramer's wife. That's all." He paused, saw that Ray was waiting for more. "What the hell do you want? I just knew her to say hello."

"You're lying."

"Look, hophead, I told you I don't have to—"

"You're lying, you son of a bitch. You saw Eileen every day."

"Sure, while she was on the band. Hell, I—"

"Even after she left the band. Even after she joined up with Scat Lewis. You saw her every day. Why?"

"I didn't see—"

Ray reached out suddenly, wrapped his massive fist in Massine's undershirt. He felt the give of the cotton as he yanked the drummer forward.

"Start talking, Massine."

"I ain't got nothing to—"

Ray's hand flicked out, slapping Massine across the cheek backhanded. "Talk!"

"You wanna play rough, hophead, I can play just as—"

The hand lashed out again, harder this time. Massine's head snapped back, and his lips tightened over his teeth. "Look, you bastard," Ray said. "I'm getting sick and tired of being the fall guy, understand? I want to know what you and Eileen did every day, and I want to know fast. I'm an impatient man, so talk. Talk *now!*"

"Make me, you—"

Ray bunched his fist and threw it, all in one liquid motion. He felt his knuckles collide with Massine's cheekbone, saw the red gash appear magically on the drummer's skin. Massine drew back his head, ready to spit, and Ray gave it to him again, hard, square in the mouth this time. The blood splashed over his knuckles. Massine's lip split open like a punctured balloon. The blood ran over his teeth, and spilled down onto his chin.

"You ready, Massine?" Ray drew back his fist again.

"I only saw her on the band, that's all. I only saw—"

The fist cut him short again. It was hard and bunched like a solid iron ball. It rattled into Massine's teeth and Ray felt the skin rip back off his knuckles. Massine's mouth was a pomegranate now, pulpy and red.

Ray pulled back his fist.

"All right, all right!" Massine shrieked. "I saw her. Damn you, I saw her."

"Every day?"

"Every day, yes, every day."

"Why?"

Massine didn't answer. He leaned against the fist bunched in his undershirt, his breath ragged and uneven.

*"Why?"* Ray shouted.

"She—she—was an addict."

"I know that." He tightened his fist in the undershirt. He was sweating, and he didn't like this. There was an insistent pounding in his head. His mouth was dry. "Come on, come on. Talk, Massine."

"I was getting her the stuff." Massine let out a tortured sigh. "Heroin. I was supplying her."

Ray's mind flicked to the sixteen ounces of heroin Eileen had shown him. His brows pulled together, and his mouth hardened.

"You're lying again, Massine. I'm going to break every tooth in your mouth unless—"

"I'm not lying," Massine screamed. He lowered his voice. "I'm not lying. Why would I lie? She was a junkie. I got the stuff for her. That's the truth. Why should I lie?"

"How much stuff? How much each day?"

"An eighth, a quarter. It varied."

Ray unleashed his right fist again. Massine's head shook with the blow, and his eyes were pleading and surprised.

"That's the truth! Holy God, it's the truth."

"Eileen Chalmers had sixteen ounces of pure heroin with her when she was killed," Ray said.

"No!" Massine's eyes were wide. Shock registered on his face.

"I saw it," Ray said. "Sixteen goddam ounces. What would she need a punk like you for?"

"Sixteen—ounces?" Massine shook his head. "No, no—" He seemed to be trying to digest the fact. "That's impossible."

"I saw it."

"Sixteen ounces? Pure?"

"I said sixteen ounces. Stop stalling, Massine."

"I don't know, I don't know. She must have just got it. So help me, I sold her heroin every day."

"You want another fistful, Massine?"

"I swear! Jesus, I swear. On my mother, I swear. I supplied her."

Ray shoved Massine backward, pulled his hand from the undershirt. "All right," he said. He began pacing the room.

It was with him again—all the longing, all the mounting desire. It tore at his mind and his body, threatened to shake his nerves loose from his skin, gouged at his stomach. And he'd thought it had left him. That was a laugh, all right. That was the biggest laugh today. It was still here, big as life, scratching away at his back. Goddamned monkey!

Massine was leaning against the table, a fresh cigarette in his mouth.

"Getting you, eh, hophead?" he asked.

There was something familiar in the voice, the subtle urging perhaps, the superior tone, the well-known inflection of the man who held the key. Ray turned swiftly, his eyes narrowed. The sweat stood out on his brow in round, shining globules.

"Massine," he said softly, his voice a hiss. Massine didn't answer. He backed against the table as Ray advanced slowly.

"You supplied Eileen."

"Look, I already told you—"

"You're going to supply me."

"What?"

"You heard me." His voice was still low. It went on in an even tone, persuasively menacing. "You're going to get me all the horse I need."

"You're crazy. The cops are checking ever pusher in the city. You think I'm gonna stick out my neck for a lousy—"

"Yes," Ray said. "I think so."

"Well, you're crazy. You think I want to spend the next five years in jail?"

"I don't care where you spend the next five years."

"Well, I do. You're the hottest thing in the city, pal. The cops find out I'm feeding you and—"

"But you're going to do it."

"No!" Massine screamed. He stubbed out his cigarette. "No!"

"I'd hate like hell to bust your nose, Massine. I'd hate like hell to do that."

"You can't hurt me no more, Stone. You just—"

"You know my name." He wasn't really surprised, but it meant that Kramer had probably told the cops about the hair dye already. Fine, just fine.

"Everybody knows your name, Stone. That's why I ain't going to risk my hide getting you no—"

"Shut up!" Ray snapped. He walked up close to Massine. "I need the stuff, Massine. I need it so damn bad that I'm liable to rip off your arms if I don't get it. You understand? That's how bad I need it. You going to get it for me, or do I start ripping? Make up your mind fast, Massine."

Massine gulped audibly, his eyes glued to Ray's face. "Sure, Stone. Sure, I'll get some stuff for you."

Ray felt a sweet pain shoot through his body. He was going to get fixed. Soon, soon. He was going to get a shot.

"Now," he said quickly.

"Take it easy, Stone, take it easy." Ray recognized the oily tones of the pusher again, and he clenched his fists. Massine said hastily, "I got to go out and get the stuff."

"Where?"

"A connection."

"How long?"

"About five hours."

"That's too long," Ray snapped.

"I told you, Stone, they got the city covered like a corpse. I can't just run out and get the stuff. It's going to take a little time."

"Two hours," Ray said. "No more." He reconsidered quickly. "Make it an hour."

"Have a heart, Stone. How can I—"

"All right, an hour and a half. No more, understand?"

Massine nodded halfheartedly. "Okay. Christ, you must think I'm a magician."

"I don't care what you are. Bring back a quarter-ounce in an hour and a half."

"A quarter! Stone, that's impossible."

"An eighth, then."

"I'll try."

"You'll get it, Massine. If you don't, I'll be waiting here to break your arms. You'll get it."

Massine nodded dully. "You better take a walk meanwhile."

"Why?"

"I just don't want any cops to catch you here, that's all."

Ray bunched his fists, took a step that brought him within three inches of Massine. "You planning a cross, Massine?"

"Hell, no. Why should I—"

"I'm just making sure. Remember this, Massine. If I get picked up in the next hour and a half, I'm going to tell the cops you're my pusher."

"What?"

"You heard me. I'll tell them you've been supplying me for the past fifty years. How does that sound, Massine?"

"Hell, Stone—"

"And I'll tell you something else. If you're not back here in an hour and a half, I'm going to call the cops and tell them all about you, anyway."

Massine tried to assume the pose of a hurt little boy. "You can trust me, Stone," he said.

"I know." Ray smiled. "You've got almost as much to lose as I have." He looked at Massine's wrist. "What time is it?"

"Five to seven."

"I'll be back at eight-thirty."

"Okay."

Ray started for the door. He paused with his hand on the knob, then turned, smiling.

"You'd better have the stuff, Massine."

"I'll have it."

"Eight-thirty."

"Sure, sure."

Ray wet his lips. An hour and a half. Ninety minutes. Ninety minutes to heaven. The thought was delicious.

Quickly, he closed the door behind him.

## Chapter Seven

Dusk touched the sky, streaking it with lavenders, reds, oranges as the sun dipped below the horizon. The neon flickers leaped into life, shouting their wares to Broadway. And the people began to come out of their holes, pleasure seekers, curious, indifferent, interested, bored. Men in shirt sleeves, and girls in light cotton dresses. Sailors in tight whites and tilted hats, popcorn vendors, floozies, be-boppers with beards and berets, a blind man with a dog and an accordion, and a drunken woman with sagging stockings and hennaed hair lying in the doorway of a photographer's shop.

Ray walked, and his eyes were bright with anticipation. One hour and thirty minutes. He wet his lips. He could almost feel the needle sinking into his arm, see the veins bulging eagerly. And then the warm spread, the sudden *sock!* and then everything would be all right. He'd be straight again.

He sighed deeply, breathing in the warm night air, feeling the breeze fresh against his face. It was spring, all right.

*"Some people need so much, Ray. All I need is springtime, and dusk, and you."*

The words rushed back involuntarily, leaping up from some shadowed corner of his mind. He could almost hear her voice, almost see the breathless way her lips had parted when she spoke the words. She had squeezed his hand tightly, and her eyes had met his for an instant. There had been honesty in those eyes, open and frank. And love. They had reached across to each other with their eyes, and their eyes alone had said everything there was to say, said it for all time.

He shook his head violently, trying to clear it of the memory. Times, had changed, things were different. There was no place for Jeannie anymore. It was over, finished.

But the memory persisted, and he couldn't remove it by shaking his head. The blue eyes were still there, and the auburn hair, soft and silky under his fingers. His mind raced back over the years—was it really years?—remembering settings, half-forgotten snatches of melodies, Jeannie in an evening gown, Jeannie in a bathing suit, Jeannie in paint-streaked dungarees, Jeannie in bed. He passed a hand over his eyes. It was no good. No good at all.

But when had he met her? His mind skirted the years. Back to a girl in a white piqué dress, with hair like living flame, and tanned legs, and blue eyes that gave a radiant look to her oval face.

She stood by the bandstand, leaning against the rail, her breasts pressed against her folded arms. They were playing "Stardust," he remembered, and the muted trumpets had pushed their lilting melody out onto the night air, there in the small park, with the dancers milling around on the concrete, and the stars wheeling overhead like a million diamonds on black velvet.

He had glanced up, seen her there, seen the look in her eyes. And later, when the set ended, he'd walked over, offered her a cigarette. Her voice was young, but it came from deep within her, as if speaking were a vital part of her, the way everything about her seemed to be.

They'd talked a little, and when the dance broke up she was waiting for him.

"I don't usually do this," she'd said. She glanced at him hurriedly, anxious for a sign that he believed her.

"I know. I can tell."

They'd walked through the park, the moon sifting its pale

light down through the interlaced branches of the trees, and he'd joked about how nice it was to be a piano player, no instrument to carry, and she said it would have been simply awful if he played the double bass.

And then they had passed a dark spot beneath the trees, and his hand had tightened on hers, and he felt the responding warmth. She was against him then, her young body trembling, the smell of her hair in his nostrils, fresh with the fragrance of soap. His lips touched her cheek, and it was incredibly smooth and soft. And all at once her lips were on his.

It had been a tender kiss. Their lips clung for a moment, moist against each other. She let out her breath swiftly, and her fingers tightened on his arm. Wildly she lifted her head, tossing her hair back. Her lips parted, and he drew her to him.

Somehow, in a city of ten million, quite by accident, they'd found each other.

He would always remember that first kiss. He'd kissed many girls since, but it would never be the same.

He gulped hard, shaking his head again. Maybe he should go back to her. Now, tonight. Maybe he should get his shot, and then…

No. No, that was just it. The shot. No, it was better this way. Forget Jeannie. Forget her.

He kept walking, a strange excitement pulsing through his body. Part of it, he knew, was anticipation. He always felt this way when a shot was coming. But another part was something else, something that had been stirred by his thoughts of Jeannie. It burned in the pit of his stomach, and he began to couple it with the shot, began thinking of it in terms of the shot, and how he'd feel after the shot. He wanted Jeannie. Christ, he wanted her. He'd always want her. Well, pal, you can't have her, his mind reminded him, so just forget it.

Quite automatically, his thoughts flew to Babs. If not Jeannie, why not Babs? Not the same, but why not? He looked for a clock somewhere. What the hell time was it anyway?

He was surprised to discover that it was only seven-forty-five. God, forty-five minutes to go. But after that… He smiled. He'd call Babs, tell her he'd see her later tonight. Later, after he'd been fixed. I'm taking you up on that raincheck, he would say. I'll be over a little later.

He started looking for a drugstore, pleased that he had pushed Jeannie out of his mind, yet still feeling a little guilty about the ease with which he'd accomplished it. Well, what the hell, he told himself, she's not right for me. But she was right for him, that was the trouble. She was the only right thing for him, the only thing that…

Oh stop it, Stone, he commanded himself. You're turning my stomach.

He dialed Babs's apartment, waiting, rehearsing what he'd say as the phone rang persistently. He let it ring a while, then gave up, feeling disappointed but a little relieved, too. He hadn't really let Jeannie down, after all. Perhaps it was all for the best. Besides, why the hell would he need a woman once he'd had a shot? What time was it?

He stepped out of the booth, looked at the big clock over the drug counter. Seven-fifty. God, but time could creep when you were waiting for something!

Well, what now? Where to now? Forty minutes to kill. How to kill them?

He thought of the dead Eileen with alarming suddenness. He hadn't forgotten her, surely? Hadn't forgotten the police? Hadn't forgotten that he'd been tagged? Forty minutes to a shot. Could he see someone in forty minutes, perhaps get a little more information?

Who? The second guy Babs had mentioned. Tony Sanders. Sure, why not? A few quick questions, then back to Charlie Massine and the waiting needle.

The telephone directory said Sanders had an apartment in a brownstone house on East 69th Street, opposite Hunter College. Ray tapped gently on the door and waited. He was ready to leave when it opened suddenly.

"Yes?" The voice was cultured, and Ray remembered that this was the Tony Sanders who'd been born with the silver spoon in his mouth. Except that it had been platinum in Sanders's case. This was the Sanders whose picture was plastered all over the newspapers every three months or so, leaving in his plane, or leaving on the *Queen Mary*, or taking his yacht south.

Ray decided to play it straight. "I'm a friend of Eileen Chalmers. I'd like to ask a few questions."

Sanders lifted a black eyebrow, eyed Ray critically. He was tall, exceptionally good-looking, with penetrating gray eyes fringed with black lashes. His mouth was narrow above a cleft chin, set with a slight sneer that came from years of being spoiled. He had an Indian's cheekbones, high and pronounced, and it was apparent from the smell of lotion that he'd just finished shaving. His shirt hung out of his trousers, and Ray noticed that only the top three buttons were fastened, the cuffs hanging loose too.

"You caught me dressing, friend," Sanders said. His voice didn't sound annoyed, only disinterested. "You can come in if you don't mind following me around the apartment."

"I don't mind."

Sanders stepped back into the room, leaving Ray to close the door. He finished buttoning his shirt, his broad back to Ray, then tucked it into the trousers.

"Well, what can I do for you?" He picked a pair of cuff links off the long buffet, deftly fastened them at his wrists.

"How well did you know Eileen?"

"Oh, pretty well." Sanders seemed engrossed in the cuff link at his left wrist.

"How well was that?"

Sanders looked up, his eyes wide, a faint smile tugging at his lips. "I knew her long before she even met Dale Kramer. In fact, we were going steady—to use the vernacular."

"Umm?"

Sanders smiled. "As you put it, 'umm.' I suppose you're wondering why a girl like Eileen would marry a crumb like Kramer, and leave a rich guy like me, eh?"

Ray found himself liking Sanders. He grinned and said, "Well, now that you mention it—"

Sanders turned his back to Ray, took a black tie off the buffet, walked to the long mirror over the sectional. "I always dress in the living room," he explained. "Bedrooms aren't for dressing; they're for undressing."

Ray grinned again, watching Sanders's hands move in the mirror.

"About Eileen," Sanders went on. "Crazy kid. Wanted to sing, can you imagine? I told her that with my money, we could hire every singer who ever showed his tonsils. Nope, wouldn't do. *She* had to sing." Sanders shrugged. "Artistic temperament. Never could understand it.

"So, Kramer came along with his music box and waved it in her face. She jumped at the chance. Exit Tony Sanders."

"Just like that?"

Sanders tugged at the tie. "Well, not exactly like that. There was all the preliminary horse manure, you understand. I'm trying to cut it short so I won't be late for my date." He looked up suddenly. "What time is it, anyway?"

Ray glanced unconsciously at his wrist, forgetting that he'd hocked his watch long ago. In embarrassment, he looked up and stuttered, "I—I—"

"Well, I'll make it. You a close friend of Eileen?"

"Well, yes and no."

"That's elucidating." He turned to face Ray, indicated the tie. "This damn thing straight?"

"Yes."

"Hate bow ties. Silliest damned things a man—"

"Was Eileen an addict when you knew her?"

"Eh? Oh no, that came much later."

"Then you knew she was an addict?"

"Of course." He grinned again. "Perhaps I forgot to mention that I saw Eileen every now and then—friendly basis, of course—right up until her death."

"Did her husband know this?"

Sanders shrugged, whipped a white dinner jacket off the back of a chair. "Never asked him."

"Just how friendly were you and Eileen?" Ray asked.

Sanders slipped into the jacket. "Here's another silly thing, these jackets. White."

"Just how friendly were you and—"

"I heard you the first time. Shall we talk about dinner jackets?" Sanders's tone still wasn't harsh. It was rather pleasant, Ray thought. But it left no doubt that he did not wish to discuss the extent of his relationship with the dead girl.

"Sorry," Ray said.

"That's quite all right." He took a gold watch from the buffet, slipped it over his wrist, glancing at it quickly. "I'm going to be awfully late, old man. If there's anything else, perhaps you'd better—"

"When was the last time you saw Eileen?"

Sanders made a clicking sound with his mouth. "Let me see." He thought for a moment, then flashed his disarming white smile again. "This will sound terribly melodramatic, but I'm afraid it was on the afternoon of her death."

"Oh?"

"Terrible, isn't it?" Quickly, he walked into the kitchen and snapped out the light. He came into the living room again, stuffed his wallet into his back pocket and said, "I hate to rush you out, old man—"

"That's quite all right. Thanks a lot for the information."

"Not at all." Sanders paused. "You never did tell me how well *you* knew Eileen."

"Shall we talk about dinner jackets?" Ray said. Sanders chuckled and pulled the door shut. The latch clicked and they started down the stairs together.


Two minutes.

Just up the steps, knock on the door.

Massine would open it. He'd go in, and Massine would give him the eighth. He wondered if he should pay for it. Maybe not. Maybe he could scare Massine again, and keep his money for another fix when he needed it.

He climbed the steps quickly, his heart thudding against his rib case. Heroin, his mind sang. Heroin.

He stopped outside Massine's door and knocked quickly.

He waited for an answer, the sweat beginning to ooze out all over his body. He knocked again, then tried the door knob. The door swung open slowly. Massine was sitting in an armchair, facing the window.

Ray closed the door quickly. "Did you get it?" he asked, his eyes bright, his tongue wetting his lips.

Massine didn't answer.

Ray banged a fist into his open hand. "Did you get it?" He walked in front of Massine and looked down at him.

Massine looked right back, but he wasn't seeing anything.

There was a neat little hole right between his eyes, and it dribbled blood down along the side of his nose and over his mouth.

Ray stared at the drummer.

"Massine? Mass—"

He was dead.

The heroin. What about the heroin? Ray glanced quickly toward the door. He should stay and look for it. A cold sweat broke out over his body.

Suppose the police—

He shook his head, and a sob wrenched through his chest. He wanted to weep, and he bit his lip to hold back the tears. So close. He'd been so close, so close, so close.

And then the fear raked his spine and he ran for the door, not looking back at the dead man staring out the window.

## Chapter Eight

He let the phone ring. Please be home, he thought.

"Hello?"

"Hello, Babs?" His voice came out in a rush.

"Yes?"

"I tried to get you before. You weren't—"

"Who is this?"

"Ray. Ray…" He stopped short, trying to remember what last name he'd given her. "Ray," he repeated weakly.

"Oh, hello!" Her voice became smooth, syrupy.

"I've got to see you, Babs. You're the only one who can—"

She laughed a rising laugh, and somehow the sound irritated him. "Slow down, honey," she said. "You sound like a machine gun."

"I've got to see you," he repeated slowly.

"Well, I've got a dinner engagement, Ray." Her voice was apologetic now.

"So late?"

"It's only eight-thirty, honey."

"Well, Jesus, can't you break it?"

"I'm afraid not."

He clamped his jaws together, ready to hang up.

Her voice came to him again. "I can see you later, Ray."

"When?"

"I'll try to beg off early. Ten, ten-thirty."

"Can't you make it sooner?"

"I'm cutting it awfully close as it is."

A new thought came to him. "What about the Trade Winds? Aren't you singing tonight?"

"No," she said. "Kramer didn't think it would look good for the band to appear the same night Eileen's murder was announced. He's arranged for a substitute band."

"Oh. All right, I'll see you at ten, then."

"Fine."

"Babs?"

"Yes?"

"Where shall I meet you?"

"My place," she said. There was a long pause. "That all right with you?"

"Yes. Yes, that's fine."

"We'll dance."

"I wanted to talk to you, Babs. I'm—"

"We'll talk, too."

"All right."

"I'll see you later then. Bye."

"So long, Babs."

He held the receiver to his ear long after he heard the click on the other end. Then he hung it back on the hook and sat in the booth.

A man walked by the glass door, and Ray glanced over his shoulder quickly. He was getting the jitters, all right. It was beginning to get him, the hunted feeling. He'd feel better when he could talk to someone. Ten o'clock, she'd said. That would be fine.

He thought of Charlie Massine sitting in the armchair, the crimson trail of blood oozing down his face. He wondered if they'd hang that one on him, too. But how could they? Unless Massine had heroin on him. Still, the connection was a remote one.

Heroin. Maybe he should have searched the place. Suppose Massine *had* gotten the eighth? A beautiful eighth of H in a dead man's pocket, going to waste.

The thought irritated him, and he dug into his pocket for another dime. He put it into the slot quickly and dialed the number from habit.

He heard a click as the receiver was lifted on the other end, heard mingled voices and laughter, the sound of glasses clinking, party noises. There was a laugh right near the phone, and then a fuzzy female voice said, "City Morgue."

It startled him for a moment. "What?" he asked.

"City Morgue, coroner speaking." There was another giggle, and he heard a girl shriek in the background.

"Is this Trafalgar seven—"

"Who'd you want, dearie?" the girl asked.

"Louie. Is Louie there?"

"Just a sec." He heard the party noises again, and then the girl yelled, "Louie!" The noises swarmed into the phone again. "Louie, telephone!"

Her voice came back to his ear again, louder. "Be with you in a minute, dearie."

He waited, and the sounds of revelry irritated him more. He fidgeted uncomfortably. That son of a bitch was having a good time, probably with some babe in the next room, drinking liquor he'd bought with the fivers Ray had handed over to him.

"Hello." Louie's voice was brusque. It was obvious that he hadn't wanted to he interrupted, whatever he was doing.

"Louie?"

"Yeah, who's this?"

"Ray Stone."

"Who?"

"Ray—"

"Yeah, yeah, I heard you. Listen, Stone, you must be crazy or something. What the hell's the idea calling me?"

"Louie, I need a shot right away. I've got the money this time."

"Mister, I wouldn't come near you if you had Fort Knox on your back."

"Louie, can't we—"

"For God's sake, pipe down in there!" Louie shouted, his voice away from the phone. Then, louder, "Make it snappy, Stone."

"I'll come up there, Louie. I'll—"

"You come up here and you'll find the cops waiting for you, chum. I don't want no part of you."

"Then meet me. I've got fifty bucks," he lied. "It's all yours, Louie. Just get me some stuff!"

Louie chuckled. "You really got it bad, eh, Stone?" He clucked his tongue.

"Louie, I'm going out of my skull. Louie, you know what it is, you've seen enough of it. I have to—"

"Tough, Stone."

"Look, can't you just—"

"Big party here, Stone. You better hang up."

"Louie—"

"Look, it's no sale. Understand? No sale. Goodbye, Stone."

"You're a bastard, Louie. A ten-carat bastard. When this is all over you can whistle if you think you're going to get any dough out of me."

"You're breaking my heart, Stone. When this is all over, you'll be either chopping rocks or frying."

"Don't be too damn sure," Ray shouted.

"Read the papers, Stone. The cops got you all sewed up. They got a Reserved sign on the chair, just for you."

"Go back to your party, you bastard," Ray said heatedly.

Louie's voice changed suddenly. "Come on, chum, have a heart. I can't stick my neck out for you."

"You think I killed her, Louie?"

"Well, I don't know."

"Deposit five cents for the next five minutes," the operator interrupted.

"You think I killed her?" Ray asked again.

"You better hang up. Your dime's up."

"Just, think this over, Louie. If I killed her, I can kill again. And you might be next, you lousy bastard."

"I beg your pardon, deposit five cents for the next—"

Ray slammed the phone onto the hook, immensely satisfied. Let the bastard chew on that for a while. Let him wonder if a slug was going to sing out from some alley on the way home from a meet. Let him mull over it.

The first moment of elation wore off quickly. Cut off your nose to spite your face. He still didn't have any heroin.

What the hell was the use of trying to fight the whole damned city? They'd get him in the end anyway.

He fished into his pocket, came up with two nickels. He dropped them into the box, waited for a dial tone, then twirled the dial once, his finger in the hole marked Operator.

"Your call, please."

"Police department," he said.

"Thank you."

What the hell, he'd end it all, tell them where he was, have them pick him up. He waited while the phone rang.

"Sixteenth Precinct," the bored voice said. "Sergeant Shanahan."

"I—"

"Can't hear you, sir."

His throat was dry. This wasn't the way. This wasn't it. They'd peg him for everything in the book.

"Hello?" the voice said, irritated. Quickly, he hung up. He'd wait. At ten o'clock he'd see Babs, tell her everything. Well, tell her enough, anyway. Then he'd see.

## Chapter Nine

He waited until ten-fifteen, giving her a little leeway, and then went to Barbara's apartment. The elevator operator looked at him curiously on the way up, and he realized for the first time that he hadn't shaved in two days, and that he probably looked like hell.

The motion of the elevator tugged at his stomach, and he thought he was going to be sick again. He held on grimly, his teeth clenched, until the doors flew open on the tenth floor. He nodded briefly, then, and stepped out into the carpeted hallway. He heard the doors slam shut behind him, hesitated for a moment while he got his bearings. He passed the potted palm on one side of the elevator bank, walked quickly to the apartment at the end of the hall.

*Barbara Cole,* the little white card said. He reached out and pressed the button over the card.

Muted chimes sounded from within the apartment, and he heard the sound of feet padding to the door. The peephole flew back, then clinked shut immediately. The door opened.

Babs held out both hands. "Ray. Come in."

He took her hands and she led him into the apartment.

"You're home," he said in relief.

"I said I'd be. I never break a date." He followed her into the dim comfort of the living room. She was wearing black slacks that clung to her. A short-sleeved cocoa-brown sweater molded the curve of her back and the high swell of her breasts.

"Hope you don't mind," she said, glancing over her shoulder. "I made myself comfortable."

"Not at all." He felt stiffly formal, and he stood awkwardly in the center of the room. Babs plunked herself down on the sofa, resting one arm on its back, propping her legs up on the coffee table. He noticed that she was barefoot, her nails painted a bright crimson.

"Well, sit down," she said. Her mouth was smiling, and her eyes regarded him with open interest.

"All right." He sat, folded his hands in his lap.

"Get you a drink?"

"No, no, I want to talk to you."

She nodded pertly. "All right, Ray. Talk."

"Charlie Massine," he said.

"What about Charlie?"

"He's dead."

Her hand dropped from the back of the sofa, and the twin black brows climbed up onto her forehead. "What?"

He nodded dumbly. "Shot. A hole between his eyes."

"Oh God," she said. Her small teeth sank into her lower lip, and her eyes seemed to cloud over. "God, God."

"He was in his room. Just sitting by the window. Dead."

"Are you sure?"

"Yes. He's dead."

He realized suddenly that something was wrong. He couldn't place it at first, and then he knew what it was. A policeman wouldn't behave this way over a dead man. He was supposed to be a policeman as far as Babs was concerned. Yet she'd expressed no surprise at his behavior.

"You know, don't you?" Their eyes locked, and she stared at him steadily.

"Yes," she said. "I know."

"Everything?"

"I know you're Ray Stone. That's all of it, isn't it?"

"No, that's not all," he said fiercely. "I didn't kill her."

"I didn't say you did."

"Well, it's there in your eyes. You all think I killed her. Well, damn it, I didn't. Do you understand?"

Her face was serious, her eyes warm, and sympathetic. "I understand."

"I've done a lot of filthy things, but I've never killed anyone," he went on.

"Nobody said you—"

"I'm an addict," he said. He paused. "You know that, don't you?"

"Yes."

"Well, addicts do funny things. I've done them all, every rotten, stinking, filthy one of them. All, you understand?" He paused again, then shouted defiantly. "You want to hear all the things I've done?"

"If you want to tell me." Her voice was soft.

"I've rolled drunks in alleys, taken every cent they had. I even struck up conversations with them in bars, nursed them along until they were really looped and then picked their pockets. I've done the same with fairies. Led them on, made them think I was on the make, and then slugged them for their rolls."

Babs sat still, one eyebrow raised, her feet out in front of her on the coffee table.

"I've pimped, too. I pimped for the professionals, and I pimped for kids who needed the stuff as much as I did. I've played the con game with more girls than I can remember, hocking the gifts they got from suckers, or just helping them spend the dough they got. We always spent it on the same thing: heroin. I've done a lot for heroin, even to stealing from my own father. I cashed in an insurance policy I took from my mother's bureau drawer. I pawned a cameo she'd had since her wedding day." He stopped, caught his breath. "I've done every-thing. But I've never killed anyone."

"I see."

He seemed to be carried on by his own momentum. "I've even forgotten some of the things I've done. I shoplifted every store in this city. I've got more clothes in hock than I could wear out in ten years. But I've never killed anyone."

"I see," she said again.

"You don't see!" he shouted. "You're sitting there like a smug little Buddha thinking what a low, contemptible—"

"Oh, shut up!" she said, her voice suddenly harsh. She swung her legs off the coffee table, stood up abruptly. He stopped short in the center of the room, stopped pacing to look at her. She walked toward him slowly and deliberately.

She lifted her face and said, "I don't give a damn what you've done, Ray Stone."

There was something new in her voice now. At first he didn't recognize it, and when he did he thought, What's the use? He looked down at her, saw her wet her lips with her tongue. Her eyes had narrowed, and the single lamp on the end table lighted their brown depths with fierce intensity.

She was standing, very close to him now, and she reached up with one hand, not speaking, and cupped the back of his neck. And then she raised herself on her toes, her breasts yielding to the hardness of his chest, her mouth seeking his. Her lips touched his gently at first, so gently, the passing of a mild breeze over a grove of willows. And then, with sudden wild-ness, she crushed her mouth against his own. Her mouth was alive with movement, her tongue an arrow of fire. His arms went around her, and his hands discovered the rich warmth of her body. Suddenly she was out of his arms, and he felt empty and cold. He followed her to the couch, surprised by his own response, alert to every subtle pang of this reawakening of desire.

He undressed her slowly, savoring the slow revelation of her body, marveling at contrast of ivory and shadow, smooth flesh and crisp hollows. When she kissed him again, his hand cupped her breast, and she went into his arms. Her body was warm, and her eyes were pleading, and once again she whispered, "I don't care what you've done, Ray Stone," and then he lost himself in her mouth and her arms and her warmth.

He lay back exhausted, her head cradled in his lap. The red coals of their cigarettes glowed in the darkness. He felt strangely content, happier than he'd felt in a long time.

She drew in on her cigarette, and the glow lighted her nose for an instant, hung in the planes of her finely sculptured face, ignited her eyes with pinpoints of fire.

"Has it been very bad for you?" she asked, her lips dribbling smoke.

"The drug, you mean?"

"Yes."

"Pretty bad," he said.

She was silent for a while.

"Did—did I make you forget it?"

"Yes," he said without hesitation.

"Really?"

"Yes, you made me forget it."

"Good."

They smoked silently, the sound of the street far below them, the medley of horns, and far across the city the wail of a fire siren, and the tooting of the boats on the river.

"What about Massine?" she asked.

"What about him?"

"Will the cops blame you?"

"I don't think so. They've no reason to."

"That's good." She sounded relieved.

"Did you know Massine well?"

"Pretty well. He introduced me to Kramer."

"Oh."

"You see, Eileen wanted to get on the Scat Lewis combo. When I found out about it, I asked Charlie to introduce me to Kramer. I sounded Kramer out about the switch, made the arrangement with Scat, and that was it."

"Then you knew Massine before you went on the Kramer band."

"Yes," she said. She drew in on her cigarette. "You know, I'd been on a few bands before, met Charlie around."

"I wonder if Massine was shacking with Eileen?" Ray said.

"Possibly. I imagine so."

"He said he wasn't."

"Well, he should know."

"You'd think Kramer would get angry about it. Or at least a little excited."

Babs sat up. She handed him her cigarette. "Put this out, will you?"

He took the cigarette, squashed it in the ashtray. "You'd think a husband would at least pretend to care."

"Kramer's no angel," Babs said flatly.

"What do you mean?"

"He's been playing around, too."

"Sound like the ideal married couple."

"Liberal thinking," she said shrugging. "You know how it is."

"Sure," Ray agreed.

"Kramer's been coming on quite strong for Rusty lately. I suspect she's his latest."

"Who's Rusty?"

"Rusty O'Donnell. She wiggles her hips at the Trade Winds. They bill her as an artistic dancer. That means strip artist in English."

"He likes her, huh?"

"She's quite something. You'd probably like her, too."

Her fingers were running idly over the muscles of his arm. His hand rested on her, and he could feel the even spacing of her breathing. She picked her head up suddenly, kissed him on the mouth. Her hand dropped, and she pulled away from him, her eyes wide, a playful smile on her lips.

"Why, honey," she said, "did you want something?"

He woke in the middle of the night. A breeze lifted the curtains at the window, and the dim reflection of the streetlights below were hazy in the darkness.

Babs lay curled beside him, the ivory of her thigh smooth and shining in the darkness.

He cradled his head in his hands. There was an incessant throbbing at his temples, a throbbing that threatened to shake his head to pieces. He wondered what time it was.

His eyes roamed the room, rested on a small clock on the dresser. Three-twenty.

He was sweating now, and he knew what he needed. He was foolish to think he could shake it. He'd never shake it. It would stay with him as long as he lived.

"Babs," he whispered.

He heard her even breathing, saw the rise and fall of her breasts.

"Babs," he said a little louder.

She stirred, rolled over.

"Ray?" Her voice was small and full of sleep.

"Babs, honey, listen to me."

"I'm listening, Ray." Her eyes were still closed.

"Babs, I've got to go."

"Go? Go where?"

"I've just got to take a walk. I've got to get outside."

"All right, Ray."

She rolled over again, one arm folded across her breasts.

"Babs?"

"Ummm?"

"Babs, please listen to me."

She turned, opened her eyes. She wore no makeup, and she looked young, protected by the sleepy veil that clung to her features. She smiled, squeezing her eyes shut tightly. "Hello, Ray darling."

She lifted her arm, rested it on his shoulder.

"Babs, I'm going out for a walk. I've got to take a walk."

She was wide awake instantly. She sat up abruptly. "What?"

"I'm going downstairs. I feel trapped here. I've got to walk a little." He swung his legs over the side of the bed, walked to the chair and began dressing. She pulled her knees up against her chest, folded her arms around them, sat watching him silently as he dressed.

"Is it very bad?" she asked at length.

"Yes. It's very bad."

"Poor baby."

"It'll pass," he said tersely. "Until the next time."

"How does it feel, Ray?"

"Oh, for Christ's sake!"

"I'm sorry, honey. I just thought I might be able to help."

"No, there's nothing you can do. Not unless you've got a deck of heroin with you."

"I'm sorry, darling."

"Don't worry about it, for Christ's sake." He was beginning to be annoyed by her voice, and by the silly things she was saying. She was starting to sound the way Jeannie did long ago, the same half-pitying, half-criticizing quality in her voice.

She got off the bed and came to him as he pulled on his shirt. She stood very close to him.

"Are you sure I can't help?"

"Yes, I'm sure." He buttoned the shirt. If he didn't get out of here soon he was going to bust wide open.

Her voice lowered. "Are you *really* sure?"

Viciously, he pushed her aside.

"Leave me alone!" he shouted.

"Ray!" She drew back as if he'd slapped her, and he saw the sudden hurt look in her eyes.

"Just leave me alone. There are some things that even a woman can't solve!"

She walked to the window while he finished dressing, the lights from the street below casting a red and green glow on her body.

He didn't bother with his tie. He pulled on his jacket and stuffed the wrinkled tie into one of the pockets. He left his collar unbuttoned. He was shivering now, even though he felt warm all over.

"I'm going," he said.

She turned. "You'll be back," she said. It wasn't a question.

"Do you want me to come back?"

"Yes. Oh yes, yes."

"All right," he said. He wondered if he should go over and kiss her. A spasm shivered up his back, and his hands started trembling.

He walked out of the bedroom, through the foyer, and out of the apartment.

When he reached the street, it hit him in the gut with the force of a sledge hammer. He doubled over on top of a garbage can, waiting, praying that the pain would subside.

When it passed, he was breathing hard, and his face was bathed in sweat. He struggled to his feet, breathed deeply, the restlessness stirring deep within him.

He began walking then.

## Chapter Ten

The rain began at four-twelve. It was a light drizzle at first, fine and cutting, driven by a strong wind. It lashed into his face as he walked, leaving his cheeks raw and cold, It penetrated his jacket, seeped into the collar of his shirt. The streets were almost empty, and they grew slick with the fine spray of the rain.

And then it began in earnest. Jagged streaks of lightning ripped their way across the sky, glaring white against the blackness. The thunder roared its hollow song, and the rain came down in huge drops, pelting the street, pattering on the pavements in furious accolade.

He lifted the back of his collar, dug his hands into his pockets. Tilting his head against the onslaught of water, he kept walking.

There was a fury to the sudden storm that matched the restless seething within him. Each thunderous boom found a responsive echo in his chest. Each twisted crackle of lightning tore through his nerves. He walked, and the thunder rolled overhead, and the lightning flashed in the sky. His shoes were sodden, and his clothes were plastered to his body. The water streamed down his face in rivulets, spilled onto his neck, rolled down his back.

In the distance, he saw two yellow eyes glaring into the night, heard the rumble of a motor. He squinted his eyes against the rain, saw the white top and the green body of a police car. The car turned the corner, headlights reaching out into the darkness.

He ducked his head, walked quickly into an alleyway, flattened himself against a door.

He heard a faint movement on his right, and then a tired voice asked, "Bad night. Want some fun, mister?"

He turned, startled. The girl wore a tight silk dress. Her eyes were cloaked in shadow, and her mouth was tilted upward in an inviting smile, a false smile that betrayed her profession. He faced her, ready to answer, and then he saw the fright jump into her eyes.

"Holy—Jesus!" she said. She looked at his face hard. He saw her wet her lips, and then step out into the rain. He watched the rapid swing of her buttocks in the clinging dress. Her high heels clicked against the asphalt as she hurried down the alley away from him. She looked back once, anxiously, then quickened her step. He listened to her footsteps die away, then shrugged his shoulders.

Did he look *that* bad? Sure, he needed a shave, but…

Quickly, he passed his hand over the stubble on his chin. It was rough, certainly, but not so bad that it would send a hooker scurrying away. Aimlessly, he looked at his open hand.

The palm was streaked with black.

What? How the hell…

It came to him all at once, and he lifted his hand to his hair, ran his fingers through it. When he pulled his hand away, the fingers were pitch-black.

The shoe polish! God damn it, the shoe polish was running in the rain.

He reached into his back pocket and pulled out a handkerchief. Quickly, he wiped his face, watching the white handkerchief turn black. With sudden clarity, he realized that his hair was probably half blond and half black now. That was great! All he needed was more attention than he was already getting.

He ran the handkerchief over his head until the cloth was completely black. He noticed the upturned cover of a garbage can, full of water. He stepped down, cupped his hands, shoveled water from the lid to his hair. His hands ran black, and he kept scooping water until the blackness turned milky gray, and then vanished completely. He took his tie from his pocket, wet the edge, and daubed at his eyebrows.

Standing up again, the knees of his trousers muddy and wet, he walked out of the alley and onto the main street again. He paused in front of the first store window he came to. Even in the semidarkness, he could see that his hair was blond again.

Ray shrugged. Was that good or bad? he wondered.

The knife twisted into his gut again, and he stopped wondering about everything. Overhead, the thunder had become muted, the lightning flashes spasmodic and halfhearted.

The street was covered with shining puddles of water now, and the light shimmered in them. The only sound was the sullen drip of a drainpipe.

Ray was tired, but he knew he wouldn't sleep that night.

He dug his hands deep into his pockets, and started walking again....

At five-thirty, he stole a newspaper from a stack lying bundled in front of a candy store.

His picture was no longer on the front page. In its place were the words: KRAMER'S DRUMMER SLAIN. Rapidly, he turned to page four. The police were just speculating, of course, but they believed this new development to be linked with the earlier death of Eileen Chalmers. There was a rehash of the first murder, and a new description of Ray, correcting the previous description of his hair coloring. Good old Dale Kramer, Ray thought. There wasn't much else, except the address of Peter Chalmers, Eileen's father, who refused to comment on either slaying.

Ray stared at the address for a long time.

Then he threw the newspaper into the gutter.

❖

The house was on East 217th Street in the Bronx. It rose like a tall, stucco crackerbox, its many windows reflecting the orange light of the dawn. Ray stood across the street, leaning against the iron fence surrounding the junior high school. It was a quiet street, none of the houses higher than three stories. Large shade trees crowded the sidewalks, giving the street the appearance of a shaded lane somewhere in the country.

A large brown-and-white dog trotted by on the other side of the street, glanced briefly at Ray, and then continued its solitary stroll. From one of the houses, Ray heard the strident shriek of an alarm clock, followed immediately by a low grumbling.

Another alarm clock burst into clamoring life, and Ray smiled. He fished a crumpled package from his pocket, dug into it for his one remaining cigarette. The cigarette was brown, stained from the drenching he'd received during the night, and he had to strike five soggy matches before he got one to light.

He had finished the cigarette and was grinding it out under his heel when he saw the man start down the driveway alongside the stucco house.

The man was tall, and he held his shoulders erect as he hurried down the rutted driveway. Ray pushed himself off the iron fence and crossed the street. The man carried a small green lunch pail, and he wore overalls.

As he neared the sidewalk, he saw Ray crossing the street.

Ray raised his head, ran up onto the sidewalk. "Mr. Chalmers?" he asked.

The shoulders pulled back a fraction of an inch, and the posture grew more erect. White brows pulled together into a defiant frown. The man's lips were tight when he answered.

"Yes?" His eyes were deep brown, so brown against the white of his brows that they looked black.

"I wonder if I can ask you a few questions, Mr. Chalmers?"

Chalmers studied Ray's face. "You're the addict," he said softly.

The words startled Ray. He wanted to turn and run, but his feet were glued to the pavement. "Yes," he answered.

"Did you kill her?" Chalmers's voice was steady.

"No."

Chalmers blinked, the lids closing rapidly over his eyes, then snapping upward to reveal the intense brown again.

"You should have." He turned his back on Ray, and his head high, started walking toward a '41 Oldsmobile parking at the curb.

"Mr. Chalmers. Wait—"

Chalmers leaned over, put a key into the door of the car. "Do you know who killed her?" he asked.

"No. That's what I'm trying to find out."

Chalmers nodded, pulled open the car door. "I don't feel a damn bit sorry for her," he said, his mouth still tight. "But whoever did it should pay."

"If you can just answer a few questions," Ray said.

Chalmers reached into his jacket pocket, extracted a gold watch. He snapped open the lid, looked at the time, then clicked the lid shut again. "I'll be late for work," he said. He put the watch back into his pocket.

"Where do you work?"

"Rogers-Mailer. Aircraft parts. Over the Whitestone Bridge. Know it?"

"No, But can I ride with you? I mean, we'll talk on the way over."

Chalmers looked steadily at Ray again. "Can't see any harm," he said. "Can't drive you back, though."

"I know. I just—"

"Well, get in, then."

Ray walked around to the other side of the car, waited for

Chalmers to unlock the door, and then slid onto the front seat. Chalmers turned on the ignition, and started the motor. He let it idle for a few moments, then pulled away from the curb. He stopped at the corner, looked in both directions, then made a right turn toward Gun Hill Road.

They rode in silence for a while. Then Ray said, "It seems you didn't like your daughter."

Chalmers kept looking at the road, his hands tight on the wheel. "Ain't a man alive who doesn't like his own daughter. Wouldn't be human if he felt that way. Only sometimes a daughter's better off dead."

"And you feel that way about Eileen?"

Chalmers nodded. "I knew it would turn out this way. I knew it from the very beginning. What can an old man say, though? A girl like Eileen needed a mother." He shifted his shoulders in a helpless gesture. "Ain't nothing an old man can tell her."

"Did you know Dale Kramer?"

"I knew him. I knew Tony Sanders, too. One worse than the other."

"How do you mean?"

"Didn't like Sanders from the first time I met him. What would a rich man like him want with my daughter, I asked myself. Wasn't hard to get an answer, either. I told Eileen to drop him, but you know how girls are. Stupid old man, she called me." He paused, turned onto the parkway, and was silent for a long time. Then, as if he'd never stopped speaking, he said, "Maybe she was right."

"But she did drop Sanders," Ray said.

"Sure. Of her own accord. Nothing I said ever helped her decide." A look of extreme contempt crossed his face. "Music! Musicians! I know all about musicians, young man. I know all about their breed. So she married one. Wanted to sing, she said. Well, she's singing now, all right. She's singing with the angels." He laughed a short, hard, brittle laugh. "Knew it all, she did. Knew all about musicians. Sure, she knew."

"When was the last time you saw her?" Ray asked.

"About two months ago. She told me all about it then. And about this other terrible thing. I threw her out. There's only so much a father can take. I told her I never wanted to see her again, told her to forget she had a father."

The toll gate for the bridge was directly ahead now, and Chalmers dug into his pocket for some change. He slowed the car, pulled up to the booth. Ray turned his head away from the policeman as Chalmers handed him the quarter. Far below him, the fog was lifting from the river.

"That was the last time I saw her," Chalmers said.

Ray nodded. That was how it always worked. That was the same reaction his own parents had had. He remembered telling them, his father first. He'd told them because he needed money, and there was no other place he could get it. That had been before he learned there were other ways to get money.

His father had threatened to kill him first. He'd ordered him out of the house. Ray had gone, of course. If his father wouldn't give him money, there was no point in hanging around. His father had come after him, tracing him through his musician friends, offering to help. That was later, of course. The imme- diate reaction was always rejection.

Until they felt sorry.

Then they always tried to help until they realized there *was* no way to help. Except with money. And how much money can you give a parasite? The cure came next. They offered the cure on a silver platter, and when that didn't work, they cut you off again, threatening to have you put away.

Ray's father was unique in that he'd actually called the

police—but he had waited until he thought his son had committed murder.

Peter Chalmers. Ray shrugged. He'd have gone through the same up-and-down, on-and-off process, too, given time. Unfortunately, his daughter had been killed before he'd had a chance to overcome his first indignation.

"Maybe I done wrong," Chalmers said. They were on the span now, the strong silver cables arching overhead like the spires of a cathedral. "Maybe I should have been more understanding. But it was a terrible thing, and I'm only a human being."

"The heroin, you mean?" Ray asked.

"Heroin?" Chalmers's eyebrows shot up onto his forehead, and then he began to chuckle softly, a bitter chuckle that was hollow and ghostly in the automobile. "Heroin? I'm not talking about that. I mean the baby. My daughter was pregnant."

"Are you sure?" Ray asked, surprised.

"Yes, I'm sure." Chalmers's voice was tired. "She was a month gone when I saw her, three months gone when she was killed."

"I don't understand," Ray said. "What's so terrible about that? I mean, she was married and all."

Chalmers laughed, and the sound died in the car before he spoke again.

"My daughter left her husband's band six months ago," he said. "And she and he were legally separated at the same time."

## Chapter Eleven

Look at it like a sheet of music, a complicated score with difficult fingering.

Start a beautiful melody called Eileen, play it light, allegro, for twenty-two bars. Then kill it.

Bring in your subordinate theme, label it Charlie Massine, start it softly, with reminiscent snatches of the main theme, bring it to a climax. Kill it.

Then pull in your beautiful melody again, and this time weave it through with snatches of underlying currents: Babs, Tony Sanders, Dale Kramer, Peter Chalmers.

Sustain a heavy bass with the Peter Chalmers motif, sprinkled with a Dale Kramer pecking at the upper register.

Start a fast-traveling, frantic boogie, label it Tony Sanders. Pull in a handful of harmonious chords, full, throbbing, lingering, and call them Barbara Cole.

Then play them all together in a violent, sombre dance of death touched lightly with sixteen ounces of heroin. Move your fingers furiously, and try to find the key.

If you're the police, add a single note, and keep pounding at it with one finger. The note is Ray Stone, hophead. That's the key.

If you're not the police, then try, just try to pin down the elusive key among the jumbled counterpoints, the erratic rhythms, the subtle melodies. Especially when you're playing a tune called "Cold Turkey," or "A Variation on Desire."

Ray sat in the back of the speeding bus, the spires of Manhattan scratching at the sky in the distance. He'd be off the bridge soon, back in the Bronx, and Peter Chalmers would be nothing more than a memory.

A memory and a new melody for the intricate composition. Eileen pregnant! Who shoots pregnant women? Cuckolds: Dale Kramer? Irate parents: Peter Chalmers?

No, the symphony was unfinished. There were notes missing. Without those important notes… Ray shrugged, wondering if there were time before the police played the last bar.

"You'll find him at the Stockton Baths," the voice on the phone had said. "Scat goes there every day about this time."

Ray stood downstairs, looked up at the big sign across the second floor of the hotel.

### STOCKTON BATHS
*Turkish Steam — Whirlpool — Galvanic — Cabinet*
*Separate Physiotherapy Depts. for Men and Women*

He walked up the long flight of steps, stopped at the desk in the lobby. A clerk, his face a bloom of livid acne, glanced up from a cheesecake magazine.

"Yes?" His voice twanged out through his long nose.

"I'm looking for Mr. Lewis. They said I would find him here."

"Mr. Lewis?" The clerk's pale-blue eyes settled on Ray's face, rested there for a moment. Apprehension clutched Ray again. He took in a deep breath now and waited.

"Yes," the clerk went on, "Mr. Lewis is in Four. Down at the end of the hall."

Ray nodded.

"You'll need a towel," the clerk said. "Three dollars, please."

Ray fished into his wallet, grimaced as he handed over the three bills. His money was going too fast. At this rate, he'd have nothing left when and if he *could* get a fix.

The clerk passed him a large towel. "Want to check your valuables?"

"Yes, I guess so. Just the wallet."

The clerk glanced at his stubble. "You can rent a razor in the shower room," he said. He yanked an envelope from a nest of cubbyholes, shoved it across the counter. "Just fill this out."

Ray signed the name "Ray Davis," stuffed his wallet into the envelope, then thought about the razor. It mightn't be a bad idea at that. "How much for the razor?" he asked.

"Fifty cents." Ray took a dollar from the wallet, then sealed the envelope.

"Lockers are on your right," the clerk said.

"Thanks."

Ray took the closest locker, undressed quickly, and draped the towel around his waist. He started off down the hall then, the subtle hiss of steam reaching his ears. On either side of the hallway, yawning tile doorways belched great clouds of steam. He stopped outside the first open doorway, wiped the moisture from the numeral set in the tile. Two.

He shrugged and kept walking. The heat was beginning to get him. He wiped the back of his hand over his forehead, pleased when he saw the numeral four outside the last door in the hall. Quickly, he stepped inside.

It was hotter here. The steam shifted about the room, swirling over the tile floor, sweeping up over the walls, hanging from the ceiling. He was beginning to sweat profusely. He felt his pores open, felt the moisture break out all over his body. Christ, it was hot!

"Mr. Lewis?" he called.

From somewhere beyond the shifting screen of steam, he heard a voice answer, "Yeah?" The voice was low, rasping.

He pushed his way through the steam, which was closing in

on him like a powerful physical force now. The sweat ran down his neck, flowed from under his armpits, streaked his arms. His beard felt itchy.

Seated in the corner formed by the two tile walls, one leg stretched out on the tile bench, the other resting on the floor, was what appeared to be a large white statue at first. Ray squinted through the steam, cleared his throat.

"Mr. Lewis?"

"That's me, man."

He seemed utterly exhausted, almost limp. His head rested against the tiles. His hands were folded across the layers of fat on his enormous stomach. The fat hung down from his arms, skin that must have been muscle once. A towel rested across his middle, and two chunky legs jutted out from its fuzzy edge.

He blinked his eyes, let his mouth fall open. The sweat streamed down his face, putting a high sheen on the flat nose and the full, flabby lips.

"They told me I'd find you here," Ray said. He felt hotter now, too hot, too damned hot. He coughed, wiped a hand over the back of his neck.

"I'm listening, man," Lewis said. He closed his eyes, and the steam swirled up around his head.

"What do you know about Eileen Chalmers?" Ray said.

Lewis didn't change his position. "Nice chick," he said. "Shame."

"Any idea who killed her?"

Lewis cleared his throat, and his lips flapped outward. "They say the junkie." His eyes blinked and he asked, "Who are you anyway, man?"

"Reporter," Ray said.

"What brings you here?"

"She sang for you, didn't she?"

"Sure, sure."

"Any good?"

"Not bad," Lewis said. "Not a Babs Cole, but not a crow, either. She could warble when the spirit moved her."

"Did you know she was an addict?"

Lewis blinked, shifted his position, the layers of fat vibrating. He pulled his towel higher, folded his hands again.

"Sure," he said. "Horse, you know." He shook his head, and his chins flapped with the motion. "Never touch the stuff, myself. A little tea every now and then—but never the big stuff. Gives me a nice sound, marijuana I mean. Makes the horn mellow." He grinned, exposing yellowed teeth.

"Tried to talk Eileen out of it," he went on. "Nice young kid like her. Hell, that stuff ain't no good, man. I think she was trying to quit, too."

"How long had she been on the band?" Ray asked.

"My band?"

"Yes." Ray was getting impatient. He rubbed at his nose, tried to blink the sweat out of his eyes. The steam folded over them, covered them like a heavy, wet blanket.

"Five, six months. Don't remember exactly. Babs came to me with the switcheroo. Says she had a chance for the Kramer outfit, says she had a singer to replace her." Lewis stopped, blinked twice rapidly. "Hey, man, you won't print what I said about the tea, will you?"

"No, no, of course not."

"Well, I said I'd have to hear the other chick first. So Babs brings her down, and she's okay, and the switch went through. Hell, I couldn't hold Babs back anyway."

"I don't follow."

"She can *sing*, man. A golden throat, you follow? Wouldn't have been right to hold her back. Be different if it was the old days." He paused, nodded his head. "You ever catch any of the old records I cut?"

"Yes," Ray said.

"*Moonglow, Basin Street Blues, Can't Get Started.* Hell, I could really blow then. A thrush like Babs would have been right there with the old Scat Lewis combo. Ain't the same no more. She's better off with Kramer."

"I see."

"I got a stand-still band, man. We ain't going nowhere but right where we are. Kid like Eileen, she just loved to warble, didn't matter where, didn't matter for who. Babs—well, she's got drive, ambition. Better off with Kramer. You see, man, I got no illusions, you follow me? I know just what I used to be, and just what I am. So Babs wanted more than the outfit could give her. I let her go. You know?"

"Sure," Ray said. Every muscle in his body felt lax, loose. His face felt tired, worn and still the steam persisted.

"Strictly a stand-still band, mine. You know?"

"Sure," Ray repeated.

"Eileen was happy with us, though. And like I said, she could really warble sometimes."

"What was your connection with Eileen?"

"I don't dig you." Lewis's voice was puzzled.

"You know, what—"

"Oh, yeah, I'm with you." Lewis began laughing, a soft chuckle that rolled upward from the layers of fat around his middle. His face was red through the steam when he answered. "Just look at me, man. There's your answer."

He laughed again. "Eileen was a young chick, pretty. Me, I'm nowhere, absolutely nowhere. In the old days, maybe, but not now. Nope, I was just an employer to Eileen. And a friend, I guess."

"What makes you think she was trying a cure? You said a little while ago that—"

"Oh, yeah. Well, she kept going to see a doctor, figured that was why."

"Which doctor? Where?"

"Doctor Leo—I think it was Leo—Simms. Got an office on East Seventy-third. You'll find his number in the book."

"Leo Simms," Ray repeated.

"Yeah, I think it was Leo. Something like that anyway."

"Leo Simms."

"Yeah." Lewis smiled. "Man, you look hot."

"Christ," Ray said. "I *am* hot!"

"Me, I could sit here all day. Really good for you, too. Gets all the bugs out of your system."

Ray wiped his forehead again. "Gets the *system* out of your system, too," he said wryly.

Lewis laughed, the layers of fat rolling and rolling.

"Well, thanks," Ray said. "You've really helped a lot."

He started for the door, anxious to take a shower and a shave. He'd need a shave if he were going to call on Dr. Simms.

He pushed through the steam, and behind him he heard Lewis shout, "You won't print that marijuana stuff now, will you?"

## Chapter Twelve

I spend my life in phone booths, he thought. Ever since Eileen was killed, I've been living inside a phone booth.

Someone's acrid sweat clung to the mouthpiece. His nose twitched as he waited, listening to the buzz on the other end.

Come on, come on!

"Hello." The voice was soft, and it rather excited him.

"Babs?"

"Ray! Darling, where are you? Are you all right? I was nearly fran—"

"I'm all right, Babs. I'm fine."

"Darling, darling, why did you leave? I should never have let you go. I didn't sleep all night. I—"

Ray grinned. "Neither did I, honey."

"Where are you, Ray?"

"I'm on East Seventy-third Street. I've got to see a doctor."

"A doctor? Ray, are you sure you're all right?"

"I'm fine, honey, considering. The doctor's not for me."

"Oh."

"All right if I come up tonight?"

Her voice lowered. "Do you have to ask, Ray?"

"I'll see you later."

"I'll leave the key with the doorman."

"Won't you be home?"

"No. I'm singing tonight. Kramer's decided to come out of mourning, the hypocrite."

"All right, I'll be over."

"Darling?"

"Yes?"

"Take care of yourself."

"I will."

"Goodbye, sweetheart."

"Bye."

He hung up, waited for the flutter in his stomach to subside. Christ, what a woman! he thought.

Dr. Leo Simms was a dignified man who looked like an older Errol Flynn. He kept his well-manicured hands in front of him, the fingers built into a small, tapering cathedral.

"And you are her brother?" he asked Ray. He cocked an eyebrow, and his face remained expressionless.

"Yes," Ray said.

"Mmm. Well, yes, Mr. Chalmers, your sister was pregnant."

Ray nodded, watching the doctor's cool blue eyes. The doctor was prematurely gray, and his hair was meticulously combed back on the sides of his head.

"How far along?" Ray asked.

Dr. Simms tapped the fingers in his cathedral together, then allowed the structure to collapse as he placed his hands on the desk. "Three months, we figured."

"When did you see her last?"

"On the morning of the day she was murdered. I was rather astonished when I saw the newspaper the next day."

A warning signal clicked in Ray's brain.

"Did she seem worried about the baby?"

"No, not at all. She asked the usual questions an expectant mother asks."

"Did—did you know she was an addict?"

"Of course. I told her she'd have to quit. I was amazed she hadn't lost the baby already. In cases like that, the mother usually miscarries between the first and third months."

"Is it possible that— I mean, was it dangerous? Being pregnant and an addict?"

"Well, it certainly wasn't desirable. You understand that the mother's bloodstream supplies the baby, too. It's rare that a child will survive under such constant exposure to stimulants. Frankly, I was anticipating a miscarriage."

"But her death? That couldn't—"

"Have been due to the baby? I hardly think so. The newspapers say there were two bullet holes in her stomach."

"Yes. Of course. I—"

"Mrs. Kramer never mentioned a brother," Dr. Simms said abruptly. "Neither did the newspapers. I've been following them rather closely. Sort of a personal interest, you might say."

Ray stood up. "Well, Dr. Simms, thanks—"

"You'd better go fast, Mr. Stone," the doctor said. "I'm going to call the police as soon as you leave this room."

"I didn't kill her," Ray said, his voice half-pleading.

Dr. Simms walked to the phone, rested his hand on the cradle. "I didn't say you did. As a matter of fact, the reason I didn't call the police immediately was that I was curious about your visit to me." He shrugged. "I'll have to call them, though. Strictly to protect myself, you understand."

"Sure." Ray turned, walked toward the big, double white doors.

"One thing, Stone."

"Yes?"

"Your hair. It's blond again. Perhaps the police won't have to know that."

Ray looked at the doctor for a long time. The doctor was smiling gently. "Thanks," Ray said. "Thanks."

He closed the big doors behind him, walked past the women with bulging stomachs in the waiting room, then stepped out into the air, the sun flashing down into his eyes.

A car pulled up to the curb, and two men climbed leisurely to the sidewalk. Ray turned, began walking toward Park Avenue.

It was a lazy morning, the kind of morning that made a guy

want to lie in the grass with his shoes off. Maybe he'd walk in the park, relax a while. Hell, there wouldn't be many cops in the park. Who'd look for a murderer in Central Park?

The idea appealed to him. There wasn't much he could do now, anyway. Ask a few more questions, possibly. But who? Rusty O'Donnell? She was Kramer's new doll, and maybe she knew something. Well, he could do that later. He was tired, and he could use a little nap. He quickened his step, suddenly became aware of the clicking foosteps behind him.

A man drew up on his left, and Ray turned his head quickly. He snapped it back when he felt strong fingers tightening on his right arm.

"Hey, what—"

"Just keep walking, Mac," the man on his left said. "Just keep walking and nobody'll get hurt."

The police! That lousy, rotten doctor had…

"That's a good boy," the man on the right said. "Just keep your trap shut and keep walking."

He clamped his teeth on his lower lip, kept walking between the two men. Somehow, they didn't act like cops.

"See that gray Buick turning the corner?"

Ray looked, saw a car pulling onto Park Avenue. It was the same car that had drawn alongside the curb as he left the doctor's office. He nodded.

"Well, we're going to get in that car," the man on his left said softly. "Just walk up to it, understand? I'll open the door and get in first. You'll get in next, and Freddy'll get in last. All natural-like, you understand, Mac?"

"I understand."

They walked over to the car, three gentlemen out for an afternoon stroll. The man on Ray's left opened the door, showed Ray his broad back as he entered. Ray climbed in after him, and Freddy got into the car and slammed the door.

"Okay," the burly man said. "Let's go."

The driver turned back, grinning. He had a toothpick in his mouth, and his nose curled down almost to his lips. His hair was slicked back with oil. "This the junkie?" he asked.

"This is him." The man on Ray's left nudged Ray in the ribs. "That right, Mac?"

"I—"

He jabbed Ray again, harder this time. "Answer when I talk to you, Mac."

"Sure," Ray said, beginning to get angry now. "I'm the junkie."

The big man's hand lashed out, catching Ray on his jawbone. Ray's head snapped back, and he brought his hand to his face, his eyes wide in surprise.

"Talk decent," the big man said.

"Easy, Hank," Freddy cautioned. "Easy."

Hank shrugged, seemed to pout off into his corner of the car. "He was getting snotty," he said. "Damn hophead."

The driver threw the car into gear, set it in motion. They headed west, hitting the West Side Highway, up the Henry Hudson Parkway, finally onto the Saw Mill River Parkway. They rode in silence, Hank's big shoulders pressing against Ray, Freddy's shoulders against his on the right.

"You're not police," Ray said.

The driver laughed, and Hank said, "You're smart, you know?"

"Where are we going?"

"You'll see."

"What's it all about?" Ray persisted.

"You talk too much," Freddy said.

Ray looked at the man. He had bright red hair, a freckled face. For a moment, he reminded Ray of the bartender at the Ace High. But there was a meanness in Freddy's eyes that killed that thought immediately.

Hank cleared his throat and Ray turned his head. He was

heavily bearded, with thick lips and a thick nose. Heavy scar tissue hugged his eyes, lidding their brownness. Ray looked at the beard, and was suddenly happy that he'd shaved.

"You'll get plenty of chance to talk later," Hank informed him. "Meanwhile, shut up."

The windows of the farmhouse were boarded up, the house itself set far back from the main highway. The car bounced and jostled along the rutted road.

"This is it," the driver said.

They were in Connecticut. Ray looked at the old red house warily. He felt Hank's elbow in his ribs again.

"Get out," the voice said.

Ray stumbled out of the car, his feet plunging into mud. Hank shoved him from behind, shouted, "Up to the house."

They walked on either side of Ray, the driver just ahead of them. The driver opened the door with a small key, walked inside and opened a window. They followed behind him.

The house was unfurnished except for several straight chairs. Thick dust covered the floors and windows, and the room smelled musty and aged.

"Sit down," Hank said. He gestured toward a chair.

"Listen, don't you think you ought to tell me—"

"Sit down!"

Ray looked up at the gun in Hank's fist. It was big and blue, and the gaping end of it stared at Ray menacingly. A .45, with big fat slugs. Not the kind that had killed Eileen and Charlie.

He sat down while Freddy came over with a heavy rope, swinging it over Ray's head and then pulling it tight over his arms. He wrapped the rope around Ray several times, looped it under the chair, and then tied each of his ankles to opposite chair legs.

"You can yell all you want now," Hank said. "Ain't nobody for miles."

Hank kept the gun in his fist, put both fists on his hips, stood in front of Ray with widespread legs and looked down at him.

"What'd you do with it?" he asked.

A frown crossed Ray's forehead, "What? What'd I do with what?"

Hank grinned. "Look, junkie, this can be easy or it can be hard. Any way you like it. You tell us what we want to know, and the party'll be short and sweet. One-two-six, all over. You want to play coy, we'll have to help you along. It'll be easier the other way. You understand?"

"Sure." Ray squirmed against the ropes that were cutting into his ankles and wrists.

"So what'd you do with the stuff?"

"What stuff?"

Hank shook his head, as if he were chiding a naughty boy. "I don't think you got my point, junkie. We don't mind a joke, you understand, but we ain't got much time. No time to waste with a punk like you, anyway. So you tell us what we want to know without any fooling around and everything'll be fine."

"I don't know what you're talking about," Ray said.

The gun came up with amazing speed, a bluish blur in the sunlight streaming through the open window. He tried to turn his head aside, but he was too late. The barrel slashed across his cheek, slapping into the bone, ripping the flesh back in a tearing flash of pain.

Ray yelled, "What the hell—"

"Where's the heroin?" Hank asked. He stood over Ray with the gun on the flat of his palm now, ready for another blow.

"Heroin? What heroin?"

The blow came, the checked walnut stock slamming into the

side of his face. Ray shook his head to focus his eyes. He wanted to touch his face to see if he were bleeding. He tried to move his hands, felt the rope bite into them.

Hank's sweating face came into view, the scar tissue white against his brown eyes. He leaned over close to Ray's face, his breath smothering Ray with tobacco and beer fumes.

"The sixteen ounces of horse. Where'd you hide it?"

"Oh," Ray said, his breath rasping into his throat. "Eileen's horse. Yeah, yeah."

"Where is it?"

"I don't know."

"Where is it?"

"I don't know, I told you."

Hank slapped Ray with his open palm.

"Where is it?" The hand sliced across in a backward motion, and the knuckles rocked Ray's head to the side.

"I don't know. Jesus, I don't know."

"You saw the stuff?"

"Yes." He felt something sticky work its way down the side of his face, ooze over his jawbone, down his neck, onto his open collar. "Yes, I saw it."

"Sixteen ounces?"

"Yes. In a tin. A candy tin."

"What happened to it?"

"I don't know. It was gone in the morning."

Freddy moved up close to Hank. "Ain't no use talking to a junkie," he said. "These slobs don't know what they're saying half the time."

Hank sighed deeply. "What'd you do with it, junkie?"

"I didn't take it, for Christ's sake. Eileen and I had a fix that night. I looked for the horse in the morning, but it was gone."

"We know it's gone. Where'd you put it?"

"I didn't put it anywhere. It was gone, I told you."

Hank sighed again, slowly took the .45 from his belt. "Well, junkie," he said. "It looks like we're gonna have to prolong the party a little." He slapped the gun against the palm of his hand.

*There were faces moving in a sea of darkness. Faces that swam into view and then faded, drowning, drowning. There was a steady battering, pounding, thrashing, rocking. Incessant. It fell on his face, the pounding, hammered at his stomach and ribs. His mouth was a gaping red wound, and there were razor blades slashing at his lips, or knives, and spikes inside his mouth, or nails, or sharp glass.*

*Something was heavy on his stomach, a Mack truck, or an El pillar, something. And white hot pliers were squeezing his entrails, searing them with flame. He wanted to scream but every time he opened his mouth, he would choke and something thick and hot in his throat would strangle him.*

*And under it all was the soundtrack, persistent, monotonous, eating through the pain like acid on steel. "Where's the heroin? Where's the heroin heroin heroin heroin heroin…"*

"I don't know!" he screamed.

"Easy," a voice said.

"He's coming out of it," another voice murmured. The voices were far away, lined with fur. They were coming from the end of a long conical cave, and there was a pinpoint of light at the far end of the cave, and the light was getting brighter and brighter and brighter and brighter.

"I don't know!" he screamed again. "I don't know. Honest, honest."

Something slapped his face. The skin was raw. It hurt when the slap touched it. The slapping continued, little pats, gentle little pats, coaxing him to awareness.

Ray opened his eyes.

"That's a good boy," a voice said.

"You been out for a long time," another voice said.

"Wh—where am I?"

"You're at the Waldorf-Astoria," the first voice said. Ray heard a laugh, tried to turn his head. He squinted his eyes shut in pain against the throbbing that shook his temples.

"I—I remember now," he mumbled.

"Do you remember where the heroin is?"

"No!" He shouted it. "I mean, there's nothing to remember. I just don't know, that's all. I never did know. It just disappeared, that's all."

"You know how long you been out, junkie?"

Ray focused his eyes, looked up at Hank's bearded face.

"How long?"

"Just about four hours. Just enough time for us to send to New York for a little present. A present just for you if you tell us what we want to know."

"I already told you—"

Hank's voice was persuasive, oily. "When was the last time you had a shot, junkie?"

"A real shot," Freddy joined in.

The driver, lounging against the wall with a toothpick still between his teeth, smiled. "Heroin," he said, announcing the word, making it sound like "diamonds."

"The night with Eil—" Ray stopped short. What were they driving at? What had they cooked up?

"How would you like a shot?" Hank asked.

"I wouldn't," Ray lied.

Hank took his hand from behind his back. He held a syringe, the glass tube glistening in the late sun, the needle reflecting tiny slivers of light. In the barrel, Ray saw the whitish fluid he knew so well. His throat suddenly went dry. He swallowed, stared at the hypo in Hank's fingers.

"There's enough in here to send you to the stars and back,

junkie. Not too much, but just enough. Just enough to quiet your nerves." He paused. "You can have it, junkie."

Ray's breath came out in short, machine-gun spurts. He sobbed dryly, his head rocking back and forth. "I—I—I don't—don't want it—don't want it—"

His eyes began to tear, and his muscles shook. His face fell apart gradually, a tic near his eye first, a muscle twitch close to his lips, a trembling of the chin. All at once, it became a shivering mass of flesh that twitched and jerked spasmodically. His teeth rattled in his mouth and he tried to shake his head, tried to turn it away from the tormenting sight of the loaded needle, waiting, waiting.

"Come on, junkie," Hank's voice went on, smooth and soft now. "You know you'd love a shot. We'll jab it right into your arm, junkie, all of it. You're a mainliner, aren't you, junkie?"

"Yes— I mean, no. I— No—" He wet his lips, tried to control the frantic heave of his chest. "Get it away, for Christ's sake," he shouted. "Get it away!" His voice trailed off into a sob.

"Sure, junkie, we'll get it away. We'll give it all to you. Just tell us where you hid the stuff."

"I didn't hide it," he screamed. "I didn't take it! I didn't, didn't. Leave me alone."

"Look, junkie."

He raised his head, the muscles in his neck jerking crazily. Hank was grinning, one hand on the syringe, the other hand spread wide, the thumb touching the plunger. "Look, junkie," he repeated.

Hank's thumb tightened on the plunger, and a short squirt of white fluid arched out into the air, formed a tiny wet line on the floor.

Ray stared at the precious liquid, looked quickly back to the rest of the heroin in the syringe. Hank's voice went suddenly hard.

"Listen to me, you son of a bitch. I'm going to squirt all this horse on the floor unless you start talking fast."

"There's nothing—nothing to say, nothing. I don't know where the stuff is. I just don't know."

"All right, you dumb bastard. Watch." He pressed the plunger again, and a longer stream squirted out this time.

"Don't!" Ray shouted.

"Where's the heroin?"

"I don't know. I don't know."

The thumb flicked again, the liquid squirting from the end of the needle. "Where is it? God damn it, where did you put it? We'll beat your silly brains out, Stone. Where's that heroin?"

Ray shook his head dumbly, too spent to speak. Hank's thumb shoved against the plunger, pushing it clear down into the glass cylinder. Ray watched the heroin arc out of the needle, squirt onto the floor, seep into the dust of the boards.

"Take him," Hank said.

Ray turned his head quickly. His eyes opened as he saw the gun butt reaching out for him. There was an explosion alongside his left ear, a fiery display of screaming stars. He struggled to keep his head up, felt the next solid blow crush into the base of his skull. He stopped struggling then.

## Chapter Thirteen

He was no longer in the chair. They had taken him out of the chair, had kicked him, had held him against the wall and pounded his stomach, on and on, over and over again, always repeating the same words, the same tiring words.

He lay huddled against the wall now, too weak to move. They were gone. It was over.

He lay against the wall and stared into the darkness, the blood caked on his face, his clothes torn and filthy. This is how it ends, he thought. Something like this. A filthy room, or a garbage-strewn alley, or a city ward full of bums.

He knew pain now, real pain. It flashed through his body like unleashed lightning, ripping at his groin, tearing at his muscles, splitting the marrow of his bones. No stomach ache this time. Hell, that was easy. That was pain an addict got used to. But this was different. This was a constant, pressing pain that drained all his strength.

They had beaten him, all right; they had promised to knock his silly brains out, and they'd done it.

He tried to stand, collapsed down into the corner as his legs gave way under him.

This is the way it ends, he thought again. Jeannie was right all along.

He stared into the blackness, the bones in his face feeling bruised and raw. He could feel the puffed swelling of his lips, the lump that threatened to close one of his eyes. The darkness was soothing, and he lay there, allowing his thoughts to roam, thinking of anything but the pain.

*

There was a breeze on the roof that night long ago. It skirted over the chimney tops, whipped up over the slanting tiles, flattened Jeannie's dress against her legs.

There were stars, too, and a slender moon that glistened in the auburn of her hair, touched her uplifted face with a yellow tint. The hair streamed back over her shoulders and she held her chin high, her dress flapping against her thighs. She was silent for a long time, and then she turned, leaned against the high brick barrier. "Ray, what is it?"

"What is what?"

"With us? What's happening?"

"Nothing's happening," he mumbled. "That's the trouble!"

"You're so—so restless. I feel as if—as if something were constantly eating at you. What is it, Ray?"

He felt like telling her. He felt like saying, "Heroin, that's what! Do you know what heroin is, darling?"

"Nothing," he said, "nothing at all. Not a damned thing."

He looked at her again, at the high rise of her breasts, the white line above the browned skin, where the dress ended and the sun had not touched her.

"I know there's something wrong," she insisted. "I can feel it."

"There's nothing wrong."

"What is it, Ray?"

"Oh, shut up!" he shouted.

"Ray!"

"You want to know? You really want to know?" He was ready to tell her. By God, he was ready to tell her.

"Yes, please. What?"

"You'd better hold your breath, sweetie," he taunted, bursting with his power now.

"Tell me, Ray." Her voice was soft.

"Sure. There's a monkey on my back, a fifteen-pound monkey and his name is Horse."

A confused flicker crossed her eyes. "I don't under—"

"Horse is his nickname. His real name is Heroin."

"Hero—"

"Sure, Jeannie, heroin. Heroin, Jeannie. You know, that nasty old drug."

"But what—"

"I've been taking heroin. For a long time now. Does that explain my restlessness? Been shooting it into my arms." He paused, then added triumphantly, "Want to see my needle? Addicts always carry one, you know. A needle and a spoon—our working tools."

Her hand had gone up to her throat. "Ray—you're kidding."

"Hell, no, I'm not. I'm an addict, sweethcart. What's more, I like it. I like it a lot."

"Ray—"

"Oh, come off it, Jeannie. I'm an addict, so what? That's the way it is. That's my habit. Some guys bite their nails—"

"Stop it!"

"Or bet the horses. I'm an addict. My habit is heroin. Everybody has a—"

"Ray, stop it!"

"Everybody has a habit," he said, a little louder this time. "Your habit is virginity." That amused him somehow, and he chuckled lightly.

He was surprised to find her in his arms. She buried her face in his chest, and he felt the hot tears stain the front of his T-shirt. He suddenly felt clumsy and big, as if he were holding a fragile china doll in his hands, unable to put it down, yet afraid he'd crush it.

"Jeannie," he said softly. "I'm sorry. I didn't mean—"

She moved closer and he felt the lines of her body through her dress, taut and firm, slender as a willow.

"Ray," she murmured, "Ray baby, poor baby, poor baby."

A look crossed her face then, and he stared at her curiously. It was an age-old look, the look of the eternal woman, a look of possession and desire, of submission and triumph.

"I want you to give up the drug," she said. Her voice was strangely harsh. "Do you understand?"

He didn't answer.

"You're my man, Ray," she said. "You've been mine for a long time now, and nothing's going to take you away from me."

"Jeannie," he said, unsure of himself now, not knowing what to say, "I didn't want you to cry, honest. It's nothing to cry about. I know lots of guys who use—"

"No, I shouldn't have cried," she said, her voice still oddly hard and brittle. "It's not something to cry about. It's something to stop." She paused and eyed him steadily. "I want you to stop, Ray. You won't need it anymore."

"Jeannie, I—"

"You won't need the drug, Ray," she said more firmly. Her voice carried to the dark corners of the roof, seemed to echo hollowly back at them, strengthening their aloneness.

He looked at her, puzzled. Her voice was flat and calm. There were tear stains on her cheeks, but her face presented a coldly rigid mask of determination, the mouth drawn into a hard, almost cruel line, the eyes bright with purpose, the nostrils wide and flaring.

Mechanically, with the cold precision of a prostitute, she slid down the zipper at the side of her dress, and then stepped out of it.

"Jeannie," he started, "what—"

"Touch me," she said. There was no warmth in her voice.

She was issuing a command, and there was something strangely compelling about her now, so that he moved toward her as if he were hypnotized.

"Give me your hands," she said.

The moon slithered from behind a cloud, touching the cones of her bra and the sloping flesh of her breasts. She took his hands and guided them over her body, moving against him. The moon was gone again, and in the darkness he felt her lips on the side of his neck, felt the deliberate, mechanical, methodical writhing of her body against his. And because she was so coldly cruel, and because she was so purposefully intent, and because there was an almost savage fervor in her, he took her wildly and roughly until she could only shriek his name again and again and again to the blackness of the night.

The darkness was all around him now, filling every corner of the room. He propped himself up on one elbow, blinked his eyes.

A body for a drug: fair trade. Except that Jeannie had got the dirty end of the stick. Nineteen years is a long time to keep a habit. She'd given herself to keep him away from the drug.

That's where she'd been cheated. He'd kept his habit.

He rolled over, got his knees under him, struggled to keep from blacking out. Slowly, painfully, he dragged himself to his feet, braced himself against the wall while he got used to the new pain of standing. He walked then, a step at a time, slowly, dragging his feet, groping for a light switch.

His aching fingers found one on the wall. The sudden glare seared his eyeballs, and he closed his eyes tightly for a few moments. He looked around, tried to find a bathroom.

Drunkenly, he weaved across the room, staggered through a

doorway, flicked on another light. He stood over the bathroom sink and looked into the mirror.

Horror-struck, he pulled back, his mouth open with a voiceless cry of terror.

That face of his. That grotesquely puffed eye belonged to him, the swollen lips, the cut forehead, the raw flesh on both cheeks, the blood dripping down the side of the nose, caked in the seams of the mouth. They were all his.

He bent to the faucets and a throbbing started under his eye. He grimaced in pain and began washing the blood from his face. The cold water stung its way into the countless cuts. He clenched his teeth. Gingerly, he touched the area around his battered eye.

He let the water drain out of the sink, daubed at his face with some toilet paper. He walked back into the large room again, his eyes noticing the blood stains on the floor.

And then he saw something else.

The metal glittered, and the glass reflected light dully. The syringe! They'd left the syringe.

He ran to it, his muscles and bones protesting. He stooped and picked it up in trembling fingers. He held it up to the light, examined the glass cylinder carefully.

A little, maybe; maybe just a little.

The craving was back. Under the other pains the craving welled up inside him.

Clinging to the sides of the glass, maybe, not much, but a little, not a hell of a lot, but maybe enough, no, never enough but maybe just a little bit, just a drop, just something.

He clutched the syringe tightly, rushed it into the bathroom. He clawed at the door of the medicine cabinet, flung it open, his eyes rapidly scanning the labels.

Iodine. Boric Acid. Vitamin B-1. Epsom Salts, Cotton Bal—

Wait, wait. Vitamin B-1. Sure, why not? Sure, that would do it. Sure, sure.

His heart sang in his chest as he melted two of the vitamin capsules.

He rolled up his sleeve and deftly, swiftly, plunged the needle into his skin.

He was covered with sweat. He swallowed heavily and waited. Nothing happened.

He waited, tonguing the oily taste of the vitamins as his blood stream carried the fluid to his taste buds. But no charge, no lift, no soaring. Nothing!

He stared at the syringe on the open palm of his hand. Then, furiously, he threw it at the wall, the glass shattering into a hundred flying pieces.

He stood on the road for a long time, his thumb cocked, trying to keep his face in the shadows. A vegetable truck stopped at last, and he hopped in. The driver looked at his face once, then turned back to the road. Neither man spoke during the long ride into the city. Ray kept staring out at the trees flashing by, at the white ribbon of road that curved through the Connecticut countryside. He thought of the beating, and why he had been beaten. He thought of the dead Eileen, and Massine, and Scat Lewis, and Tony Sanders, and Dale Kramer. He thought of Babs and the warmth of her, and how her body felt lying beside his.

"I'm goin' all the way down to the market," the driver said suddenly. "You wanna go that far?"

"Huh?"

"I said I'm—"

"Well, where are we now?" Ray asked.

"We'll be in the city soon."

"Oh. Well, just drop me where it's convenient."

"Sure."

They rode a little while longer in silence, entering the Bronx.

"Been in a scrap?" the driver asked. His voice wasn't prying. He sounded interested.

"Yes," Ray said.

"Thought so."

The driver didn't ask any more questions. He kept his eyes on the road, his big, brown hands steady on the wheel.

"I'm going to Eighty-second and Park," Ray said. "Anywhere near there will be fine."

The driver nodded. "Drop you on Eighty-sixth and York," he said. "You can get a crosstown bus from there."

"Thanks."

"Don't mention it. Hate to make the long run alone anyway."

They drove deeper into the city, heading downtown. The streetlights clicked against nonexistent traffic. The city slept.

On Eighty-sixth, the driver pulled over to the curb. Ray hopped out and stood on the sidewalk for a moment.

"Thanks again," he said.

"Better take care of that eye," the driver answered.

The little truck coughed and pulled away from the curb. Ray stood watching it as it traveled down the empty street. He started walking up toward First Avenue then.


He held his finger on the buzzer. Within the apartment, the chimes sounded again and again, melodious, loud in the still-ness of the early morning.

He heard the snap of the lock, and then the door opened a tiny crack. A brown eye appeared in the crack, and then the door swung wide. He stepped in quickly, and the door closed behind him. He turned to face the door again.

She was leaning back against it, her eyes closed tightly in

thankfulness. She wore a pajama top, nothing more, and her legs curved out beneath it.

"Thank God," she murmured. "Oh, thank God." She pushed herself off the door then, came into his arms, her eyes still closed tightly. Ray held her close, drowned himself in the scent of her, drank in the sleepy warmth of her. Her body was vibrantly alive beneath the silk pajama top. He held her away from him and looked at her closely, studied the wild disarray of her black hair, the oval loveliness of her face, pale now without makeup, her lips swollen and ripe.

"Come," she said. She slipped out of his arms and took his hand, walking into the bedroom.

She sat down on the bed, and he sat down beside her. She reached for the lamp on the end table and snapped it on.

She turned, and her eyes opened wide in shock. "Ray! Good God, what did they do to you?"

She reached out with a slim, cool, hand and he flinched. The pain shot into his eye again. He winced and she took his head in her hands, brought him close to the warmth of her body.

"Darling, darling," she said. "Tell me what happened."

"I got a working over. But good. I think I know now why Eileen was killed."

"Tell me, darling. Tell me."

"They wanted to know what I'd done with the heroin. The lousy bastards kept on even after I told them—"

"Who, Ray? Who were they?"

"I never saw them before. I told them I didn't know what had happened to the horse, but they kept hitting me anyway. Hank, one was called. And Freddy."

"Go on."

"I think they killed her for the stuff, Babs, They must have. Why else would they pick me up and pound hell—"

"But that's nonsense, Ray. If they had the stuff, why would they beat you?"

"Something must have got fouled up along the way. But that's why she was killed, all right. I'd bet my life on it."

She was stroking his forehead now. "You'll need some sleep," she said. "Forget all this, Ray. Get some sleep and we'll talk about it in the morning."

"I found out something else, too," he said, "just before they picked me up."

"Darling, don't try to talk."

"I'm all right, Babs. A little sore, but all right otherwise. Eileen was pregnant, did you know that?"

"I like you better as a blond, did you know that?" she asked.

He touched his hair. "The rain— It washed out the black."

"Go to sleep, darling," she said. "Close your eyes." He nodded, suddenly exhausted. In a few moments, he was dead asleep.

## Chapter Fourteen

Ray woke to the accompaniment of a tympany pounding away inside his head. The sun poked through the blinds with long yellow fingers. Dust motes floated lazily on the air, visible in the strong sunlight.

He thought of the needle first. No matter where he was, no matter what condition, his first waking thoughts were of the needle.

There was the familiar tenseness tugging at his nerves, the empty feeling in the pit of his stomach, the hot ball of lead in his throat. The merry-go-round never stopped. You took a ride, and as soon as you were rested you took another ride.

And every morning, rain or shine, hell or high water, your nerves beat out a Dixieland dirge, blaring at your senses, shrieking, screaming. Until the fix. The fix smoothed everything out, spread oil on the troubled waters, calmed the nerves, stopped the clamorous beating inside the skull.

There was no fix this morning.

There'd been no fix yesterday morning, and none the morning before that, either. Had it been only three mornings so far? Something must be wrong with the clocks. Time must have called it quits for a while. Eileen had been dead for weeks, hadn't she? Hadn't it been weeks ago when he found the slugs in her belly? Hadn't that been weeks and weeks ago? Or years?

He swung his legs over the edge of the bed, remembering for the first time where he was. He glanced over his shoulder at the empty bed, the shape of Babs's head still in the pillow. An electric clock on the end table said eleven-fifteen.

"Babs?" he called.

He waited for an answer, puzzled when he got none. He began to get a little nervous, clasped his hands together and stood up abruptly. Why do addicts take everything so damned seriously, he wondered. So she doesn't answer. Maybe she's in the john, or maybe she went down for some bread or eggs or something. Why do addicts immediately assume the worst?

He knew the answer, of course. So many things could happen to an addict when he was high. It was like coming up from another world, and each time you came up you checked to see that the old world hadn't changed while you were gone. He shook his head, walked over to the bathroom door. The door was closed, so he rapped on it gently with his knuckles.

"Babs?"

There was no answer. He rapped again.

"Honey, you in there?"

Fear, sudden and sickening, ripped at his guts. He stopped breathing for an instant, heard the gallop of his heart beating against his ears.

*Three mornings ago!*

He'd wakened then, too. He'd spent the night with a girl, a lovely girl. He'd wakened and she was dead and her blood was running all over her stomach.

He twisted the doorknob violently. He stumbled into the room, glanced at the floor, the empty tub.

He let his shoulders slump then, exhausted, and let out his breath in a long, relieved sigh. He had expected to find her lying there, a bullet under her breast perhaps, or a stocking knotted around her throat. He shook his head thankfully now, chiding himself for having been such a fool.

He found the note in the kitchen, propped up against the chrome toaster. Her handwriting covered it in an excited, wide scrawl:

*Ray, baby,*

*I didn't want to wake you, darling. Forgot to tell you last night that Kramer called a full band rehearsal for this morning at ten, damn him. I'll be back as soon as I can. Please don't leave the apartment. Eggs, bacon and milk in refrigerator. Coffee in white cabinet. Bread in oven.*

*Wait for me, darling. I'll have something for you.*

The note was signed with a large "B." He read it through twice, and his eyes paused on the last sentence: I'll have something for you.

Now, what the hell did that mean? Was it her way of saying she'd throw herself into his arms the minute she got back? Or did she mean something else?

He shrugged the thought away. Where the hell would she get heroin? But maybe that's what she *did* mean. He wet his lips. Maybe she was going to bring him a deck. Maybe two. He'd wait. He'd wait if it took her ten years.

He walked back into the bathroom and looked at his face in the mirror. The puff under his eye had gone down, leaving a multicolored area the size of a baseball around the eye. He touched it with his fingertips. Well, at least it didn't hurt anymore. It sure looked like hell. Something like rotten meat. All he needed was a few maggots.

He kept staring at his face, looking at the raw areas on each cheek, the split lip. Brother, what a mess. If he ever met that son of a bitch Hank on the street, there was going to be *another* dead citizen in New York.

He let the water run, and tried piecing the thing together while he washed.

Eileen was killed for the heroin, of that he was certain. But what about Charlie Massine? Where the hell did he fit into the picture? Maybe Charlie killed Eileen, swiped the heroin, and then was killed by someone else who wanted the stuff.

He appraised this as he washed his face carefully.

His imagination ran free, quickly composing a picture of the murder. *Charlie sneaks up to the room, opens the door. Ray and Eileen are lying on the bed. Charlie pumps Eileen full of holes, picks up the tin of heroin, and leaves.*

He rinsed his face and thought this over again. No, something was wrong there. He tried it again. *Charlie comes into the room, looks for the heroin. He finds the heroin first, and then shoots Eileen. He leaves.*

Something was still wrong.

Ray reached behind him for the towel, patted his face. Assuming that the killer was after the heroin, a new problem presented itself. Why in hell was Eileen killed?

They'd both taken enough horse to keep them out for hours. There was the slim chance, of course, that Eileen had snapped out of it while the murderer was in the room, and he'd had to kill her to keep her quiet. But in all probability, Eileen was out like a light when the heroin was snatched.

So why kill her?

And if the killer disposed of *her*, why not dispose of Ray, too?

Well, the answer to that one was obvious. Whoever had killed Eileen figured that Ray was a ready-made patsy. Kill them both, and the police would still be looking for someone to pin it on. Kill only the girl, and the police would tag the guy who spent the night with her. All right, it was logical to kill only Eileen and leave Ray to take the rap. But that still didn't answer the first question: Why kill Eileen at all?

Ray squeezed some toothpaste onto his finger and briskly massaged his teeth and gums. He rinsed his mouth and walked into the bedroom to dress.

*Eileen was pregnant.*

He was used to the idea by now, and it no longer shocked him. All right, she was pregnant. So what? So a million things. The killer was the baby's father. He didn't want to marry her, so he came up to rub her out quickly and quietly.

The killer was Eileen's husband, furious at the thought of his wife pregnant by another man. He came up in a fit of jealousy and killed her.

The killer was Eileen's father, disgraced by his daughter's shameful actions.

The killer was Eileen's ex-beau, disturbed over her marriage, allowing his hurt to fester, and finally taking it out on her with two quick slugs in the gut. The killer was anybody.

That's just about what it amounted to. Except that the heroin was stolen. That meant that whoever killed Eileen wanted her dead and also wanted the heroin.

Ray shrugged into his shirt, began buttoning it up the front. It wasn't until he'd completely buttoned it that he noticed it had been washed and ironed. Quite a woman, Barbara Cole. He looked down at his trousers. They'd been wrinkled and shapeless last night when he'd thrown them over the chair. This morning, they had knife creases down both legs. He picked up his jacket and examined it closely. It, too, had been pressed, and the blood stains taken out of it.

He sighed appreciatively and tucked his shirt into his trousers, trying to pull his mind back to Eileen's death. Perhaps Charlie Massine was the father of the child. All right, Ray thought, let's take it from there.

The murderer killed Eileen in a rage. He killed Charlie in the same heat of passion. That pointed to Dale Kramer. But why should Kramer be jealous when he had a doll of his own? Rusty O'Donnell, Babs had said. Ray would have to see her, too.

But even assuming that Kramer had killed both Eileen and Charlie in a rage, where did the heroin come into the picture?

Whoa, whoa, he told himself. He had automatically assumed that Charlie and Eileen had been killed by the same person. It didn't have to be that way at all. Why, Charlie could have killed Eileen, and then been killed himself in reprisal.

Ray shook his head. There were too many possibilities, too many combinations.

Hadn't Kramer accepted his wife's death just a little too calmly? And didn't Sanders seem a little too casual about the whole thing?

Everyone had built a solid wall of protection around himself, covered the wall with indifference. But these people were Eileen's life, and she was a part of each of their lives. It seemed unnatural that her death could be shrugged off so lightly.

Someone had killed her, effectively and thoroughly. That someone had also swiped a sixteen-ounce tin of heroin. And that someone may also have killed Charlie Massine.

Tie those together into a neat little package and he should have the answer. One and one make two. They always did.

Except, in this case, one and one made zero.

He roamed around the apartment after breakfast. He hadn't eaten heavily because he was afraid it wouldn't stay down. He drank a small glass of orange juice and a cup of hot coffee. He washed the glass, the cup, and the saucer, and then began waiting for Babs to return.

The piano in the living room came as a shock to him, and he wondered why he hadn't noticed it before. He walked up to it slowly, stood looking down at the polished keys. His forefinger poked timidly at middle C. A little off, his ear told him, but a nice clean tone.

He pulled back the seat, sat down on the cushion, and pulled himself closer to the instrument. He rested his fingers on the keys lightly, like a blind man reading Braille. He didn't try to play. He just sat there with his hands on the keys, his head slightly bent, his eyes focused on the middle octave.

Tentatively, delicately, he tried to recall the fingering of "Long Ago And Far Away."

Was the key B flat, or E flat? Or had the band played it in C? B flat, E flat, C. Was that the right chord? It seemed right, the feel seemed natural.

He struck the three notes together, then poked out the melody with his right hand. Yes, it seemed right. The next chord? The fingers on his left hand hovered indecisively over the keys. He found the notes, struck too loudly. He tried for the melody with his right hand, pleased when he hit the correct sequence of notes.

But what came next? He became abruptly aware of the sweat covering the backs of his hands. He rubbed them on his trousers, then passed a hand over his wet upper lip.

Doggedly, he played the first two chords again, his mind groping for the next chord in the progression.

*Really makes you play, don't it, man?*

The memory gave him a start. Phil Ragow, wasn't it? The bass man on the band. Was that his name? Was that how it all started?

He dimly remembered an Irish wedding, with a beaming groom and a dark-haired bride. There were kegs of beer at the far end of the hall, and little ham sandwiches, and people dancing, and kids running between the dancers. It was a hot summer night, and his trousers stuck to his legs, irritating his crotch. The piano was tinny and out of tune, the keys yellowed and chipped. He remembered that two notes were completely dead in the middle octave. F and A. He couldn't play decently, and that had annoyed him. That and the noise and the set of numbers they'd just played.

Phil Ragow, if that was his name—it had been so damned long ago, and he was such a kid—hung over the big double bass like a drunk clinging to a lamppost.

"Big drag, ain't it?" he asked.

Ray nodded, the heat reaching up onto the bandstand with clammy, stifling fingers.

"Come on with me, man," Ragow said. "We'll give this little party a boost."

They went to the men's room, a urine-smelling, beer-smelling cubicle. Ragow had taken out the deck of cocaine, and Ray watched him while he went through the process of arranging it on a small hand mirror in a little white mound.

"Go on," Ragow said. "Take a sniff."

Ray hesitated. He'd tried marijuana before, but that was small-time. This was the big stuff, the inner circle. Cocaine, heroin, opium, morphine.

"Come on, man," Ragow insisted. "Build yourself a dream."

"I don't know, Phil—"

"Look man, don't be a crow. You dig this stuff and those crazy jerks out there won't be able to touch you."

Ray reluctantly admitted to himself that the heat and the noise and the frantic movement were beginning to wear on him. But still…

Ragow insisted. "Just this once, man. Can't do you no harm. Hell, all the other cats are onto it, too. Come on, come on, let's ride."

Ray sniffed. Gently. On the mirror the mound looked bigger, its reflection doubling its size.

"Hell, that ain't gonna do nothing," Ragow said. "You gonna

snort, you got to really snort. Come on, take a big pull. Come on."

Ray inhaled. The white flecks leaped off the mound, darted into his open nostrils.

"More, man. More."

He inhaled again, and the mound disintegrated. The mirror caught light from the bare bulb over the closed cubicle. The light sent splinters chipping off the surface of the mirror and Ray sniffed deeply. The mirror grew brighter, and the white mound seemed to reach up for his nose.

The noises outside the locked door of the toilet blended together into a soft, steady hum, punctuated with hoarse laughs. Ray's feet were off the ground. He was floating. He felt wonderfully light, marvelously happy.

"Hit you, eh man?" Ragow asked.

Ray grinned foolishly, blinked his eyes and then opened them. Ragow was sniffing at a new mound on the mirror.

"Christ," he said.

"Jesus H.," Ray said, the smile still on his lips.

"Mmmmm-mmm."

Ragow flushed the toilet. The noise was faraway and muted, like the wash of the ocean on a long, white beach. There were gulls over the beach, wheeling and screeching. The sky was an endless blue, cloudless, a lone white sail against the horizon.

"Let's go, man," Ragow said. "Let's go play now. Let's go play."

The kids still ran over the dance floor, but they ran slowly and their voices were hushed. Ray walked among them, grinning, floating leisurely up to the bandstand. The faces all around him were stupid, and he felt good and wise and self-sufficient. The heat no longer bothered him.

His fingers wandered over the keys during the next set, grew into the keys, became a part of the instrument, and his soul flooded out through his fingertips, and the music became a part of him. He felt wonderful. He felt just grand.

"Really makes you play, don't it, man?" Ragow asked.

He sat at the piano in Babs's apartment, and the keys were wet and slippery under his hands. He shoved back the stool abruptly and began to pace the room, thinking of that first cocaine lift, thinking of the heroin that followed.

He stopped near the piano, smashed his fist down against the keys. The cacophonous blast hung on the air, and he turned and walked back to the couch, over to the bar, back to the piano, crossing the room, recrossing it, while the sweat stood out on his brow, drenched his back. His hands trembled and his face shook, and the walls began to close in on him.

He had to get out of there. He had to walk, had to get some air.

He fairly ran to the bedroom, threw his jacket onto his back. He'd come back later, after he'd walked this off. He'd leave a note for Babs. He went into the kitchen, fumbled in one of the drawers for a pencil. When he couldn't find one immediately, he gave the idea up, walked quickly to the front door and stepped out into the hallway, clicking it shut behind him.

He pressed the elevator button, walked a short distance away from the elevator, then returned, and pressed the button again. He paced while he waited, pressed the button three more times, kept pacing.

Where the hell was the elevator? Man could die here on the goddam floor waiting for an elevator.

He punched viciously at the button, waited, then gave up in despair. What floor was he on? Tenth, yes, tenth.

He'd walk down. Time the elevator came, he'd be chewing

up the carpet. He found the stairwell, and ran quickly down the steps. Nine, eight, seven, down, down.

He stopped to catch his breath on the third floor, then continued down to the main floor. He had half a mind to give the operator hell. Maybe he'd do just that. Go over to the guy and say, "Look, you stupid bastard. What does a man have to do to get a little elevator service?"

He spotted the door marked *Lobby,* reached for the knob and pulled it open.

His heart gave a sudden leap, and he slammed the door shut quickly. He wanted to scream. He slammed his back against the door and closed his eyes shut tightly.

Cops!

Scores of them. All over the lobby. Like cockroaches springing out of the woodwork, blue cockroaches with drawn pistols.

He waited until his heart beat normally again, then opened the door a crack, and peeked out.

No wonder he couldn't get an elevator. The cops were piling into every car. There were cops everywhere he looked, cops at the entrance to the building, cops at the switchboard, cops in and behind every chair, cops leaning against the pillars.

Ray closed the door gently, looked quickly up the stairwell.

The roof was a long way up, but it was his only chance.

## Chapter Fifteen

He started up the steps. He took them two at a time, swung around on each landing without pausing. When he reached the third floor, he heard the door down below slam shut.

"Hey!" a voice called. "This way. He's on the stairs." He heard the pound of feet on the stairs below him, began climbing faster.

"That him, Frank?" another voice called. "Come on, come on."

"He's on the stairs, Donnaly," the second voice shouted. "Get the boys to cut him off."

Ray kept climbing. He passed the fifth floor and was tempted to stop and catch his breath. The steady thud of feet behind him changed his mind. His breath tore into his chest as he labored up the steps. Behind him, he heard more feet.

"He can't go far, Frank. Door to the roof is locked."

"We'll get the bastard," the first cop answered.

Locked! They were bluffing. They were trying to get him to give up without trying. The lousy bastards were throwing a bluff. He paused on the sixth floor, looked over the railing down the stairwell.

He yanked back his head as a shot boomed from below. Quickly, he began to run again. There was noise above him. He snapped his head up rapidly, saw the door on the seventh floor landing burst open just as he reached it.

He threw his shoulder against the door, felt it crash against flesh on the other side. He backed away and the door flew open again. The cop stumbled into the hall, his pistol out in front of him as he staggered forward off balance. Ray brought his hand up and down in a quick chopping motion. The knuckle bone and hard edge of his hand hit the back of the cop's neck. He chopped again as the cop fell forward, a surprised, shocked look on his face. His gun clattered to the floor. Ray picked up the gun, a .38 Smith & Wesson Police Special.

He leaned over the railing and shouted, "I've got a gun, you bastards! Keep away from me." To emphasize his point, he fired two shots overhead.

"Watch it, men, he's armed," a voice shouted.

"He's armed, men. Careful," another voice repeated.

He started up the steps again, pleased with the sound of hurried consultation below.

Eight. How many more? How damned far to the roof?

He kept climbing, the footsteps beginning again behind him. On the tenth floor, he fired another shot over his head, heard the excited, angry voices rise in protest.

Eleven.

He almost collided with the door of the roof. It was made of metal, painted brown, and a large padlock held the door to the door frame. He aimed the Police Special at the lock, triggered off a quick shot. He drew his knee up, kicked at the door with the flat of his foot. The lock snapped and the door flew open, shooting dazzling sunlight into the darkened hallway.

He ran out onto the roof, the sound of footsteps close now, too close. He reached the ledge, glanced down. Christ, that was a mean drop. There was a sound at the door to the roof, and he whirled quickly and fired blindly. A blue-coated figure ducked inside.

Three shots to scare them on the stairs. One into the lock. One now. That left one. Great.

He climbed onto the ledge and gauged the distance to the

next building. A good six feet. He glanced hastily over his shoulder, saw a cop poke his head around the doorway again.

Poising himself on his toes, he looked over at the other building again. Far down in the street, he could see the automobiles, black beetles in the sun. He could see the white tops of the police cars, too—larvae against the black asphalt street. He dipped at the knees, tucked the .38 into his belt.

"Stop or I'll shoot," a voice shouted.

"Go ahead!" Ray shouted back. He leaped into space, his arms stretched out ahead of him. His fingers caught the ledge of the other roof, and his knees scraped brick. A shot rang out behind him, as he pulled himself over the ledge. Another bullet chipped brick three inches from his face, sending red splinters against his nose. He dropped to the tar, and inched across the roof to the opposite ledge.

They were shooting in earnest now. The bullets struck the soft tar with sullen thuds, sending thick pieces of black leaping into the air. Ray reached the second ledge, lifted his head quickly. A bullet whistled through the air, and he ducked automatically. He crawled to a red-brick chimney, circled behind it. One of the cops was climbing onto the ledge of the roof he'd left, ready to leap across. Ray pulled the .38 from his belt, triggered off a fast, overhead shot. The cop yelled out in fear, unharmed, and toppled backwards into the arms of the other waiting policemen. Ray grinned and moved to the ledge, tucking the empty .38 back into his belt. He climbed up, still protected by the chimney behind him. He leaped out, caught the opposite ledge and pulled himself up immediately.

He ran hastily across the roof, his heels sticking in the wet tar, the wind cool on his cheeks.

He had crossed two more roofs before the cops jumped the first one. He darted into the first open door he found and ran blindly down the steps. On the third floor, he dropped the .38 into a trash basket.

When he reached the street floor, he walked calmly through the lobby and out onto the pavement. A police car passed by outside, heading for Babs's apartment house. His heart leaped into his throat, but he kept walking calmly.

A cab idled at a hackstand on the corner. Without looking toward the cluster of police cars down the street, Ray opened the door near the curb and stepped inside.

"The nearest drugstore," he said, trying to keep his voice even. "And make it quick."

The book listed a Mary O'Donnell in Washington Heights. She was the only woman listed in a long line of male O'Donnells, and Ray figured he'd take the chance. Mary, Rusty.

He stood outside in the hallway now and pressed his finger against the buzzer. An ominous hum sounded within the house, and he took his finger off the button and waited.

A peephole in the door clinked open, and he could make out a brown eye behind the grillwork.

"Well, a man," a clipped voice said. "Battered and bruised, but a man."

The door opened almost immediately after the peephole clicked shut. Ray stepped back a pace. His mouth fell open.

She was small. She wore a dressing gown that curved outward over amazingly full breasts for her size. The thin silk hugged her hips, and a belt gathered the material around a narrow waist. If this was Rusty O'Donnell, they'd named her wrong. Her hair could never be called rust, never in a million years.

It was a fiery red that haloed the oval of her face. It came as a shock because her eyes were dark brown, and her brows were pitch-black. The eyes slanted upward, heavily fringed in black. Her nose was small, slightly flat.

He found his tongue at last, while the girl regarded him steadily, staring at his discolored eye.

"Miss—O'Donnell?"

"Yes?" The voice was high and clipped.

"Rusty O'Donnell?"

"Yes, of course." There was a twang to her voice, an almost sing-song lilt.

"I—"

"You're surprised?" she asked.

"Well—"

She grinned, two dimples popping into the smooth line of her cheeks, her crimson lips pulling back over small white teeth. "Don't be embarrassed," she said. "There aren't many O'Donnells who are Chinese."

"It's just—well—"

"Come in, come in." She looked at him again. "What happened to your face?" she asked.

He touched his face. "Little accident." She nodded briefly.

He stepped into the foyer, looked past the beaded curtains into the comfortable living room. Rusty closed the door behind him, walked past him. He noticed the rounded, muscular calves of her legs in the black, high-heeled pumps.

"I was dressing," she apologized. Her voice had a childlike, questioning quality. "People are always surprised," she said, still smiling. "They expect a buxom Irish lass, and they get a delicate China doll."

She laughed and added, "Of course, I'm not as fragile as most. My father was as Irish as they come. Pat O'Donnell was his name, and they didn't make Marines any tougher."

A glimmer of understanding flashed onto Ray's face.

"You've got it, my friend," Rusty said. "Seduced poor Mom

in the shade of an old pagoda." She clucked her tongue sympathetically, the smile still playing on her lips. She began to jiggle her foot, the heel of the shoe dangling from her rounded arch.

"What newspaper did you say you're from?" she asked.

"I didn't," Ray answered.

"That's right, I guess you didn't. I always assume I'm being interviewed." She paused, one arm stretched out along the back of the couch, the foot incessantly jiggling. "Well, never let it be said that Rusty O'Donnell turned any man away from her door—but just what is it you want?"

"Information," Ray said.

"Then you are a newspaper man."

"Not exactly."

"What does that mean?"

Ray thought of his picture splashed over the front page of every tabloid in town. "Let's say I work closely with the newspapers."

"All right, let's say it. Now, what kind of information do you want?"

"Is the hair real?"

"What?"

"Your hair. Is it—"

She laughed again and uncrossed her legs. "Don't be silly. It's a rinse, of course. You'd be surprised how many billings this hair gets me, Mr.—Mr.—"

"Davis."

"Mr. Davis. A Chinese girl with bright red hair. Knocks them dead." She paused and eyed Ray thoughtfully. "Have you ever caught my act?"

"No."

"Shame. It's pretty good, if you like that sort of thing." She smiled archly. "Most men like that sort of thing."

Ray grinned thinly. "Did you know Eileen Chalmers?" he asked.

"Oh, no!" she exclaimed. "Not again!"

"I—"

"That's all right, Mr. Davis. It's just that everyone seems to ask the same questions over and over again. Yes, I knew Eileen."

"Well?"

"Fairly well. No great friendship, if that's what you mean."

"Did you know Charlie Massine?

"Yes, of course."

"Was there anything between them?"

"Who?"

"Charlie and Eileen."

"Oh, of course not. Charlie and Eileen?" She began laughing. "That's absurd."

"Why?"

"Well, they're just not—compatible, I guess you'd say. No, Mr. Davis, never. Never."

"I understand you've been seeing a lot of Dale Kramer lately."

Rusty paused to reflect. "Yes, we work at the same club."

"How long have you known him?"

"Only since I began working at the Trade Winds."

"And how long is that?"

"My, you have a lot of questions." She slid down on the couch. "About four months, I guess."

"Did you know Charlie before this?"

"Yes."

"How long?"

"Charlie Massine, you mean?"

"Is there another Charlie?"

"Well, there are a lot of Charlies."

"I mean Charlie Massine."

"I've known him for years."

Ray's features expressed surprise.

"I played the Borscht Belt with him," Rusty went on. "I had

black hair then, and they billed me as Toy Willow." She smiled and added, "Toy Willow! Can you see that?"

"Charlie had his own band?"

"Why yes. Kramer played the—" Rusty cut herself short.

"Kramer played what?"

"Nothing."

"Did Kramer play with Charlie in those days?" Ray was leaning forward now. Rusty sat up and tucked the gown around her.

"Did he?" Ray insisted.

"Yes," she said. Her voice was small.

"Why'd you say you just met him then?"

Her eyes flared as she leaned forward. "Because I'm sick and tired of everyone snickering behind their filthy hands about us. I knew Kramer, so what? Maybe we even had a romance then, so what? Eileen was a tramp, and everybody knew it. So why all the fuss about what Kramer and I did or are doing now?"

"No fuss," Ray said softly.

"All right, then." Her anger seemed to subside as she leaned back against the cushions again.

"How long ago was this?" Ray asked.

"I don't follow."

"The Borscht Belt."

"Oh. Six, seven years ago. I don't remember." Her eyes whipped Ray's face. "Toy Willow was another girl, Mr. Davis. Rusty O'Donnell never thinks of her."

"I see. This band was Charlie's?"

"Yes, I told you it was. Kramer played piano for him."

"I see." He considered this a while; then he asked, "I wonder how things got reversed."

"Well, the band split up a few years after that."

"Oh? Why?"

Rusty paused, seemed to ponder whether she should go on or not, then shrugged one shoulder and said, "Massine had to leave suddenly. An appointment with the state—two years with free room and board."

"Prison?" Ray asked.

"Yes."

"What was his crime?"

Rusty shrugged again. "Possession of narcotics with intent to sell."

Ray nodded. "Well, that ties in. Anybody caught with him?"

"A lone wolf, far as anyone could tell," Rusty said. "He went to jail like a clam, and Kramer took over the band. When Charlie got out of jail, Kramer hired him as a drummer."

"I see. And you?"

"What do you mean?"

"Are you officially connected with the band?"

"No, no, I'm a free agent. I just happened to be booked into the same spot." Her black eyebrows lifted slightly and she asked, "Did you say you'd never seen my act?"

"Sorry," Ray said.

"You should be sorry. You're really missing something. The columnists call me Red China—I'm that sizzling. Stop in at the club some time. You'll see."

"I will," Ray promised. He rose. "Thank you, Miss O'Donnell."

"Not at all," she answered, walking him to the door. "I'm always happy to meet the press."

## Chapter Sixteen

Things were beginning to unravel a little, he thought. He stood outside the door to Kramer's apartment, his finger pressed to the pearl circle of the buzzer.

He didn't move his finger at all, kept leaning on the buzzer with the clamor of the hum sounding loud within the house. He was ready to give up when he heard the soft swish of feet on a thick-pile rug.

The door opened and Kramer exclaimed, "Stone!" He started to push the door shut, but Ray kicked it hard and it flew back.

Dale Kramer was wearing a blue silk dressing gown. His feet were in brown leather sandals. His green eyes were bleary, and the pencil-line mustache under his nose looked somehow awry. His skin was chalk-white, pulled tight over high cheekbones.

Ray slammed the door and leaned back against it. A smile tilted the corners of his mouth.

"Hello, Kramer."

Kramer was looking at his face. "You got the beating you deserved, I see." He turned his back on Ray, walked directly to the telephone. Ray was beside him before he could pick up the receiver. He clamped his hand over Kramer's and said, "Don't be a damned fool."

"I'll give you ten seconds to get the hell out of here," Kramer said.

Ray shoved Kramer roughly away from the phone. The bandleader clenched his fists, stood glaring at Ray.

"What do you want here, Stone?"

"Information."

"You came to the wrong place. This isn't a public library."

"I didn't come for corny gags, Kramer. I want to know why your wife left your combo."

"That's none of your business."

Ray grinned. "It is my business, Kramer." He fished a cigarette from the fresh package in his pocket, hung it on his lip. "I happen to stand accused of her murder."

Kramer gave a short, grating laugh. "That's funny, Stone. Very funny."

Ray lit the cigarette, blowing out smoke. "What?" he asked.

"That 'accused' routine. You playing the hurt, innocent child. That's very funny."

"Somehow it doesn't quite gas me," Ray said.

"Come down," Kramer snarled, his lip twisting back over his teeth. "I know you killed Eileen, and you're not fooling anyone with your song and dance."

"You're really brilliant, you know?" Ray said. "You're following the line of reasoning every stupid bastard in the city is following. That's very smart."

"I think so."

"Sure. Did you ever stop to wonder why I'd want to kill your wife? Did that ever enter your empty head?"

"Hopheads don't need reasons," Kramer said flatly.

"Ahhh, the secret word. Hophead." Ray's features twisted into a grimace. "That explains everything, doesn't it?"

"I know junkies, Stone. My wife was one, remember? I know how utterly irresponsible they can be."

"Is that why you tossed her off the band?"

"I did nothing of the kind," Kramer flared. "She left of her own accord."

"Why?"

"That's none of your business."

"You already said that."

"I'm saying it again. And I'll keep right on saying it."

Ray stepped closer to Kramer. In a conversational tone, he asked, "How would you like to lose a few teeth?"

Kramer snorted. "You don't scare me, Stone. You'd have to kill me. If you left me alive, I'd call the police the minute you stepped outside that door."

"I might leave you in no condition to call the police."

"You're tough, all right," Kramer said. "It takes a lot of guts to kill a woman!"

Ray lashed out open-handed, his palm catching Kramer on the side of his face. Kramer's head rocked back, and he stared at Ray sullenly.

"Don't say that again," Ray warned. "Don't say it ever again."

"Tough guy," Kramer muttered.

"Why'd she leave the band?"

Kramer didn't answer. He kept staring at Ray.

"Was it because of Rusty?"

"What? How—"

"I met the dragon lady," Ray said. "Is she the reason Eileen took a fast powder?"

"Rusty had nothing to do with it," Kramer said evenly.

"Then maybe you'd better tell me just what did have something to do with it."

"I've got nothing to say to you. The cops'll pick you up eventually, Stone. You can't hope to hide from the entire city."

"I don't expect to. But when they get me, I'm going to have a lot to tell them. And when they start questioning my motives, it's not going to look so hot for you."

Kramer turned away, in exasperation. "Just what the hell are you talking about?"

"The baby."

"I told you Rusty had nothing to—"

"I'm not talking about your baby doll, Kramer. I'm talking about Eileen's baby. The baby she was carrying."

Kramer's face seemed to crumble. His eyebrows climbed onto his forehead, and his eyes seemed to glaze over. "Wh— what?" he stammered.

"Didn't you know?" Ray asked. "Your wife was three months pregnant."

"You're a liar."

"She was pregnant, Kramer."

Kramer lunged across the room, his hands reaching for Ray's throat. Ray sidestepped quickly, shoved Kramer past him. Kramer turned, his teeth bared, his eyes blazing hatred.

"You're a liar!" he bellowed.

His fingers found Ray's throat, strong pianist's fingers that tightened around the Adam's apple.

"Let go!" Ray gasped.

"Take it back," Kramer shouted, strength pouring through his arms with maniacal intensity. "You lousy hophead, take it—"

Ray's hands flew up inside Kramer's extended arms. He brought them apart suddenly, his knuckles crashing against Kramer's wrists, breaking the lock on his throat. He bunched the fist of his left hand, brought it down in a hard chopping motion that caught Kramer on the side of his neck. Kramer clutched at Ray's jacket, and Ray slammed his right fist into the bandleader's gut. Kramer dropped to the rug.

"Liar," he muttered. "Dirty, hopped-up liar. Lousy son-of-a-bitch liar."

"You can check with a Dr. Leo Simms," Ray said. "You'll find him in the phone book."

"You're lying," Kramer said. This time his voice didn't carry as much conviction.

"Call the doctor, go ahead. I'm telling the truth, Kramer."

Kramer stared at Ray for a long time, as if trying to digest what he'd just said. He began to nod his head slowly then, up and down.

"I should have known," he mumbled. "I should have known from the beginning."

"What?" Ray asked.

"That fat, filthy bastard," Kramer said vehemently. "That's why she wanted to leave the band. So she could be near him all the time. That's why. I should have known."

"Who the hell are you talking about?"

"Lewis, that's who. Scat Lewis." Kramer got to his feet rapidly, moved up close to Ray. "He did it, Stone. That lousy bastard did it."

"You're dreaming," Ray said.

"It was Lewis," Kramer shouted. He clutched Ray's chest. "Go after him, Stone. Go after him and kill the bastard. He's the one who shot her. He got her in trouble and then killed her. You've got to get him, Stone."

Ray moved away from Kramer. "I thought you said I killed her."

"No, no," Kramer said hastily. "It was Lewis." He shook his head. "Can you picture that fat bastard touching Eileen? With those fat fingers? That fat, greasy—"

"I can't picture it," Ray said flatly.

"I should have known," Kramer went on. "How could she do this to me, Stone? With him? Of all people, with him? A fat, rotten—"

"You're making me sick, Kramer. Stop ranting like an outraged male. You were playing around, too."

Kramer pawed at Ray's jacket again. "But Lewis?" he said. "Can't you understand, Stone? A man like Lewis, with Eileen!"

"You're on the wrong track. Lewis couldn't—"

"Then why else would she leave the band?" Kramer asked. "Tell me that. Why else would she leave my band?"

"I can think of a few good reasons," Ray said.

"Why? Why would she?"

Ray pulled away from Kramer's grip, turned his back and started for the door. "Maybe she didn't like you very much," he said. He paused. "Maybe she realized you were nothing but a spineless cockroach." He opened the door, and threw a withering glance at Kramer. "Maybe that's why she left you."


Scat Lewis threw back his head and laughed, and the fat under his neck quivered like jello.

"Me? Me? Why, man, that's the laugh of the century." He let out another loud guffaw. "That's the greatest since the Pyramids."

He wore a white shirt, open at the throat, the sleeves rolled to his forearms. Behind him, the record player threw a hot trumpet solo into the small room. Record albums were stacked high behind Lewis's easy chair. Magazines were scattered over the floor, old copies of *DownBeat*, a few current issues of *Show Business* and, incongruously, a battered copy of *Étude*. The cigarette tray on the arm of the chair was overflowing with half-smoked butts, and an inch-long butt hung from Lewis's puffy lips.

"Her husband seems to think you were making it together," Ray repeated.

"He's blown his wig, man. Me and Eileen? Now, does that sound sensible?" Lewis shook his head and leaned back. A tenor sax picked up the melody, and Lewis cocked his head to one side. "Dig this ride, man. Listen to the sound he gets."

"Did you know Eileen was pregnant?" Ray asked. He studied the trumpet player's face. Lewis's lips parted slightly, and he widened his eyes as if it were a great effort.

"You leveling?" he asked.

Ray nodded.

"Well, now, ain't that something?" Lewis looked at Ray again. "You're not snowing me, are you?"

"She was pregnant."

Lewis nodded vaguely. "So that's why she was seeing a doctor." He shook his head, his eyes rolling. "And I thought she was trying to ditch the habit. I kept telling her it was for the birds, and I thought maybe she was listening to me. Should've known better." He looked up at Ray. "Really pregnant, huh?"

"Kramer says you were responsible."

"Ahh, man, have a heart," Lewis said. "Eileen and I never so much as held hands."

"She was a mighty pretty girl," Ray said.

"Sure, sure. Don't I know it? But a chick like Eileen doesn't have to mess with a broken-down horn man. No, man, Kramer's way off base."

"The fact remains," Ray insisted.

"Yeah," Lewis said. "Damnedest thing, ain't it?" He paused and tugged at the loose flesh under his jaw. "You check with Charlie Massine? He may have been the guy."

"Massine is dead."

"Sure, I know. I mean before, though. If anyone had the opportunity it was Charlie."

"How do you mean?"

"Hell, man, he was getting her the stuff she needed. A chick'll do most anything to get her fix. You don't know how it is with a dope fiend, man."

"I've got some idea," Ray said.

"Sure, Charlie could've done it easy."

"Pass the buck," Ray said.

"How's that?"

"Everybody's passing the buck. Kramer says you're the man, and you tag Charlie. I wonder who Charlie would pass it to."

"Ain't no way to find out, is there?"

"No."

Lewis chuckled a little, then tilted his ear toward the record player. "Listen to this, man. This is me on trumpet."

The clear, bell-like tones of a trumpet in the upper register sliced into the room. Ray listened for several moments, politely holding his tongue.

Finally, he asked, "Do you have any idea where Charlie was getting the stuff?"

"The heroin?"

"Yes."

"No idea at all, man. Most pushers don't talk about it."

"I know one who might," Ray said.

"Huh?"

"Never mind. Thanks a lot for the information."

Lewis was leaning back now, his eyes closed, his fingers drumming on the chair arm in time to the music.

"What's that?" he asked.

"Thanks. Thanks a lot."

"Not at all. Glad to help, man."


Ray waited patiently while the phone rang. There was a lot missing, but things were beginning to fit into place. He was still a long way from knowing who'd killed Eileen, but at least he no longer felt so damned confused, so helpless.

"Hello."

"Louie?"

The pusher recognized his voice. "Listen, Stone, I don't want to tell you again. I haven't got anything for you. Nothing at all. I ain't gonna—"

"All I want is information, Louie."

"What kind of information?"

"What do you know about Charlie Massine?"

"Nothing."

"Come on, Louie. He's dead now. You can tell me."

"Did you kill him, Stone?"

"No."

Louie paused, and Ray could hear the faint crackle of electricity on the line as he waited.

"He was a pusher, Stone. That's all I know."

"Would you happen to know where he got his stuff?"

"No, I don't know."

"The same place you got it?"

"Hell, no."

"How do you know?"

"I'm small-time, Stone. A few steadies like yourself, and that's the extent. Massine was connected with a big outfit."

"One more question, Louie."

"All right, Stone, make it fast. I don't know why the hell I'm bothering—"

"How much is sixteen ounces of heroin worth?"

"The cut stuff? Or pure?"

"Pure."

"Christ, a fortune. Why?"

"Just wondering. Thanks a lot, Louie."

"Yeah," Louie said.

Ray hung up and sat in the booth for a few minutes. He got up then and walked out into the street. He'd learned a little bit, but the pusher's voice had upset him. Deep within him, he could feel the restless clawing begin. He didn't know whether it was Louie's voice, or the fact that this was about the time of day he usually took a shot. But it was beginning again, taking control of his body.

He walked aimlessly, the need for the drug drumming inside him. He tried to take his mind off it, tried to think of other things, of the puzzle before him, of Babs. But it was more than mind. It climbed up through his veins and scratched at the inside of his skull. It clawed at his back and raked at his stomach. It pushed sweat out onto his skin, and it made his legs feel heavy, his heart beat faster.

He was turning a corner when it hit him with the force of a pile driver, ploughing into his midsection like a steam-powered piston. He backed against the wall of the building, his fingers frantically clutching the bricks.

He was drenched. In ten seconds, he had become soaking wet, the sweat seeping through his underwear and his shirt. He closed his eyes tightly and waited for the pain of nausea to subside, rocking his head with each roaring wave. The pavement tilted and tried to shake him off, and he clutched at the bricks for support. His scalp felt itchy, and his feet were like lead, and there was a hot iron ball in the pit of his stomach.

He hung onto the building for dear life, the sickness tugging at him like a strong undercurrent, wave after wave of nausea rolling through his stomach.

He was very sick.

He leaned against the door jamb, and the push button swam before his eyes. He didn't know how he'd found his way here. He vaguely remembered stumbling through the streets, the sun a sinking red ball on the horizon.

"Babs," he mumbled. "Babs."

A crest of blackness swept over him and he reeled, almost falling backwards. The door opened.

He was aware of her lips rounding into a surprised O, of her brown eyes opening wide, the lashes long and dark. She put an arm around him and he leaned against her gratefully as she pulled him into the apartment. His head rolled to one side as she took off his jacket and led him to the bathroom. She closed the door behind him and he was alone with the pale green tile and the bowl that moved all over the floor. He ducked his head, and the room swam, and sickness suddenly became a foul, wretched thing that stuck to the lining of his throat and sent his stomach wildly looping....

He showered afterwards. He took off his clothes and passed them out to Babs, and then he stood under a hot needle-point spray that sent stabbing fingers of sensitivity to every muscle in his body. He toweled, and wrapped the soft white square around his waist.

Barefoot, he walked back into the living room and took a cigarette from the tray on the coffee table. Babs watched him light it.

"A little better?" she asked.

"Yes, much."

She watched him intently, and her face was serious. "You shouldn't have come here, Ray. You were very foolish."

"I'll leave in a little while." He found her eyes and held them with his own. "I didn't have any place else to go, Babs."

"It isn't that, darling. I'm thinking of your own safety. The police were here all afternoon. They kept asking questions until I thought I'd scream."

"Who do you suppose tipped them?"

"I wish I knew," she said.

"What did you tell them? The cops, I mean."

Babs leaned over, reached for a cigarette, hung it on her lip and lighted it before answering him. "Nothing. Not a thing. I told them I'd never heard of you before, and that you certainly had never been to my apartment."

"Did they believe you?"

"I don't know. Probably not. That's why you were foolish to come here. They're probably watching the place."

Ray shrugged, took a long pull on his cigarette.

"What's the difference? They're watching everywhere."

"Well, you're here now," Babs said. She leaned back and her hair cushioned the back of her head against the sofa.

"It really hit me, Babs. Like a knife in the gut, I needed a shot so bad I thought I'd drop dead on the spot."

"Sit down, darling," she said. She patted the sofa beside her.

He touched the towel with the flats of his palms. "The towel—it's wet."

"The hell with the towel. Sit down."

He shrugged and sat down beside her, and she took his hand in hers and leaned her head on his bare shoulder.

"Did you know Charlie Massine was a pusher?" he asked suddenly.

She didn't move her head, and when she spoke her breath was warm against his flesh. "I suspected as much."

"Well, he was."

She wrapped one arm around his chest, pushed her head more tightly against his shoulder.

"It's one hell of a rat race," he went on. "There are so many loose ends, so many blind alleys. I keep asking people questions, but I'm not sure I'm asking the right ones—and I'm not sure the answers mean anything. All I know is that I've got to find the real answer before it's too late. That was a close call this morning, Babs. I won't be lucky always."

"What kind of questions have you been asking?"

"Oh, all kinds. I'm just trying to get a lead, something to go on. I don't ask anything definite because I've got nothing definite to ask. It's not as if I had a clue, Babs, a handkerchief with someone's initials, or hair in a comb, or anything like that. I've just got a bunch of people, that's all."

"Which people?"

"Kramer, Lewis—" He paused. "What do you know about Lewis, Babs?"

"Not very much, I'm afraid. I was only on the band a short while."

"Well, what?"

"A has-been, mostly. Used to play a great horn, but drink put an end to that. He coasts along now, on his name and his reputation. He doesn't play much, anyway. Mostly just fronts the band."

"And that's all?"

"That's about it, Ray."

"What about Tony Sanders? Do you know him at all?"

"I've dated him a few times."

"Oh?" Somehow, Ray didn't like that. He felt a knot of resentment in his chest, and he struggled to keep his voice even. "Have you seen him recently?"

"A few days ago. I had dinner with him. Why?"

"Just wondered." His forehead creased into a frown, and she sat up abruptly and looked directly into his face.

"Why, you're jealous!"

"Don't be foolish."

"You are, too."

"What's there to be jealous about?"

She giggled and pushed her hands against his chest. "Nothing. But you're jealous—I can see it in your face."

"Sanders went out with Eileen, too, didn't he?"

"Yes, he did." She had stopped giggling.

"How often did he see her?"

"Not too often."

"Did he know she was pregnant?"

"I have no idea."

Ray shook his head in disgust. "All blind alleys. Every last one of them."

"Forget them," Babs said.

"I'm tired of it," he said frankly. "I've been on the go all day. First the cops and then a hundred people. None of them know anything. None of them care."

"Who'd you see?" Babs asked.

"Rusty O'Donnell first, and then Kram—"

"Oh, you met Rusty?"

"Yes."

"What did she have to say?"

Ray shrugged. "Not a hell of a lot. I was surprised she's Chinese. You didn't tell me."

Babs's voice grew suddenly cold. "You didn't ask me."

"Ummm. Well, we talked around a little, and then I left."

"What did you talk about?"

"Oh, I don't remember. Kramer, I guess. Yes, Kramer and Eileen."

"How long did you stay?"

"Oh, a little while."

"What happened?"

"Nothing," he said, puzzled by the tone of her voice.

Babs rose suddenly, walked across the room and leaned on the liquor cabinet. "I'd be damned surprised if nothing happened." She bit off the words.

"I'm telling you, we talked. What did you ex—"

Babs's eyes flared, and her lips skinned back over even white teeth. "You're a liar."

"What!"

"Did she do her little dance for you? I understand that's her specialty. She lures little boys into her opium den and wiggles at them sideways."

"Babs!"

"No wonder you're tired." She gave a hard little laugh, throwing her head back.

"Babs, I didn't say I was tired. I just—"

"Get the hell out of here!" Babs said.

"What?" He blinked at her, puzzled. "Hey, what's—"

He reached for her, and she shoved out at him, her hands flat against his chest. He stumbled backward several paces, staring at her curiously.

Her voice was dead cold now. She seemed to be a different person standing before him. Fury glowed in her eyes, etched the hard line of her mouth.

"From one woman to another, eh, Ray? Regular Casanova, aren't you?"

"For God's sake, Babs, listen to me! I—"

"What makes you think I'll share you with her? What makes you think I'll share you with any woman?"

"Babs, I—"

She slapped him suddenly and viciously. "Get out!" she screamed. "Get out!" She ran into the bedroom, and he heard the lock click on the other side of the door.

"Babs!" he shouted.

Her voice was sweet when it answered. "You can find your way out, can't you, darling?"

"Babs, don't be ridiculous."

She didn't answer.

"Babs!"

He waited outside the doorway for a long time. Finally he realized she wasn't coming out while he was there.

He walked into the living room and dressed slowly. Once more, before he left the apartment, he called her name.

She didn't answer.

## Chapter Seventeen

He walked the streets, his hands in his pockets, his shoulders hunched.

Dusk was a faint wash against the sky. The late workers were scurrying toward the subways, their faces studiously indifferent.

So this is how it ends, he thought.

Wham, bam, thank you ma'am. It was nice knowing you, and it was swell and all that, but goodbye, my friend, and good luck, and drop dead. Period.

It seemed to him now that his life had been a series of goodbyes ever since he'd hopped on the merry-go-round. He'd broken with his parents first, and then his old friends, and then his music, and then Jeannie, and now…

The goodbye with Jeannie had been a classic. Hearts and flowers in the background, and the smell of magnolia blossoms, the lonesome shrill of a train against the night. He tried to make fun of it now, but somehow it didn't quite come off that way. He could remember the scene vividly, could almost reach out and touch the objects in the room. The two roses in the tall vase on the table. The white wisp of curtain that lifted and fell with each dying breeze. The white terry robe Jeannie had wrapped around her. Her hair bunched at the back of her neck, tied there with a green ribbon, smelling of soap, smelling clean.

The breeze had been warm, a breeze that carried the distant sounds of the city with it, the hurried footsteps on the pavement below, the impatient honking of the taxis, the jingling of the ice cream truck's bells.

She stood by the window, and her head was slightly bent.

She had one arm raised against the window frame, and her eyes were looking down at the little park across the street—but he knew she wasn't seeing anything.

There was that peculiar silence in the room, with the traffic sounds muffled and obscured in the distance, a summer silence bred of heat, tense with the hushed expectancy that descends upon a city before an electric storm.

"It's no go," she said. She kept her head turned, her eyes averted from his.

"What? What's no go?" He was straddling the kitchen chair, staring at her intently. It was hot, and his armpits were wet, his face sweaty.

"Us, Ray."

Silence occupied the room again, pushing into every corner. He heard the drip of the tap splashing against an upturned glass. Behind that, like a subtle counterpoint, was the ticking of the white-faced clock over the stove.

"Okay," he said.

She turned quickly. "You don't understand, Ray. It's not what you're thinking."

He shoved his chair back, the scraping harsh and grating. "I understand, Jeannie. We don't have to go into it."

She tried to smile, but her eyes were wide and glassy-looking. He saw tears behind them, and he wished she wouldn't cry. He couldn't stand it if she started crying.

"No, Ray, I don't think you'll ever understand. Oh, I know what you're thinking. The rat deserting the sinking ship, isn't that it?"

"Something like it," he said. He had the peculiar feeling that he was no longer a part of what was happening. He had stopped participating the moment she'd said it was no go. From then on, he was only watching, a mildly interested spectator watching two strangers go through a curious ritual.

"That isn't it at all," she said.

"All right, Jeannie. Let's just forget. We'll shake hands, and I'll leave, and that'll be—"

She went on talking as if he'd never interrupted. "You see, Ray, if I cared less it wouldn't matter at all. That's the trouble. I care too much." She tried to smile again, and the smile stuck to her face like a mask.

"Look, Jeannie—"

"My first love. You're my first love, Ray." She bit her lips. He knew the tears were close now, and he wanted to get out of the room. Beyond the window, beyond the rooftops, out over the river, the sky was turning gray, tremendous billowy clouds piling up on the horizon. The breeze was stiffer now, and the curtain flapped against her arm as she stood by the window. "That sounds corny, I know. People have first loves in kindergarten. They get over them."

She turned, and her eyes were wide, with her brows pinched together, and her lips parted in anguish. "This was it for me, Ray. First love with all its heartaches, all its wonderful discovery. You. That was enough. Just you, and that was all. The beginning and the end. You. Everything was you."

"Jeannie—"

"Please, darling. Let me talk. I know I've lost you now, and that's why I'm letting you go. I'm being selfish, but not because I want to, Ray. I just—I just can't take it anymore, it's like watching a dream die, watching it crumble before your eyes, sink into the dust, vanish. Ray, Ray, you don't know how it is, watching you and—and the drug. I—I can't do anything. I can't stop it, can't tear it out by its filthy roots, trample it, step on it, kill it. I watch. I just watch, and I see you and my love for you and it rips out my insides until I want to die."

"Jeannie, for God's sake, let's just—"

"That's the way it is, Ray. First love. You're supposed to be hurt the first time, aren't you?" She turned to the window again, and the first drops began to fall from the sky, pattering silently on the roof, drumming against the pavements.

"It's raining," she said.

"Yes."

She stood watching the slanting rain, the sky asphalt now, the steady tattoo filling the small room.

"So that's it," she said at last. "We'll live, I suppose."

"We'll live," he repeated blankly.

"They say you always love hardest the first time. They say that your first love always stays with you, buried somewhere in a dark corner of your heart. It'll be that way with me, Ray. No matter what, it'll always be that way with me."

He didn't say anything. He walked softly to the door and opened it. A fresh gust of wind swept across the room, lifted the curtain, ushered him out. She was standing with her back to him when he left, looking out the window.

Beneath the steady patter of the rain, he heard her quiet sobbing…

He walked now, and he thought of Jeannie, and of the things she'd left unsaid. She hadn't mentioned the money he'd taken from her, or the money he'd stolen. She had kindly forgotten all about the sapphire ring he'd taken from her jewel box and hocked. Or the luggage. Or the wristwatch. She had never mentioned the fact that he had once brought a drunk to her and asked her to spend the night with him. She had slammed the door in the drunk's face, and then held Ray tight to her breast while the shivers of addiction had ravaged his body. She never mentioned that.

First love.

She picked a fine one, all right. The first one should be the best. By all rights, it should be the very best, the indoctrination, the initiation into the mystery, the one to remember. It should be the one to look back on, the one that cherished memories of hay rides or roller coasters, or Fifth Avenue buses, or lazy Saturdays on the beach with twisted straws in empty coke bottles and white, white teeth and browned faces. The first one should be all excitement and eagerness and youth and laughter. Seagulls against a pale blue sky. A distant sailboat. The first love should be...

First love. Your first love always stays with you. He stopped short. Why sure, sure! If your husband is playing around, you look elsewhere. But you don't go to your pusher, and you don't go to your present employer. You go to your first love!

Not Charlie Massine, then. And not Scat Lewis!

By Christ! By the good holy Christ.

Ray began running.

Hunter College was decked in its spring finery. The evening session students, slim, long-legged girls in silk dresses, sat on the side steps, their skirts tucked coyly under their shapely buttocks. Ray glanced briefly in their direction, then walked into the lobby of Tony Sanders's house. He climbed the two flights to Sanders's apartment and rapped loudly on the door.

The door opened almost instantly, and Ray backed away in surprise.

An astonished look crossed Sanders's handsome features. "Oh," he said, "it's you."

"Mind if I come in?"

"Well, friend—"

Ray shouldered his way past Sanders, walked into the living room. "Hope I didn't catch you dressing again," he said.

Sanders passed a hand over the cleft in his chin. His indolent mouth registered no emotion. His gray eyes were placid.

"No," he said. "Not quite. I'm pretty busy, though, and I'd appreciate it if we could make it for some other time."

"I'm pretty busy, too," Ray said.

"Well, I'm afraid that's not much concern of mine."

"I forgot to ask you a few questions last time."

Sanders shrugged his broad shoulders. He wore a white shirt open at the throat, tucked meticulously into gray flannel slacks. "All right, ask your questions. But please make it fast."

"Eileen was pregnant," Ray said.

"I know. Is that meant to be a revelation?"

"You said you saw her the day she was killed."

"Yes, in the afternoon." Sanders gestured impatiently. "Look, friend, I thought you had new questions. It seems to me we covered all this ground the last time you were here."

"Partly," Ray said. "Eileen went to see her doctor that morning. Then she saw you in the afternoon."

"Well, what of it?" Sanders began kneading the big knuckles of one hand with the palm of the other.

"Kramer thinks Scat Lewis was the father of the child. If you know Scat Lewis, you'd understand how foolish that premise is."

"Come on, let's get on with this. If you've got any questions, ask them."

"Lewis thinks Charlie Massine was the impetuous boy. Eileen was an addict, and an addict will do most anything for a shot. But Massine was a businessman—and a roll in the hay isn't a roll in the bank. Eileen may have been willing to shack with him for a shot, but I doubt if Massine would have settled for anything less than hard cash."

"All of which explains your theory that Massine wasn't the father, either," Sanders said, derision in his voice.

"Right. You're the father."

Sanders didn't explode. He began chuckling instead. He

walked to the bar and raised the top, resting it gently against the wall. Carefully, he unscrewed the cap of a Scotch bottle and poured himself a hooker, without offering one to Ray.

"You've got a sense of humor, all right," he said. He lifted the shot glass to his lips, tossed it off quickly.

"I've got more than that. I should have realized it all along. You were the logical guy. Good-looking, rich, charming—and her first love. The shoulder to cry on. The comforting heart."

"I still find all this very amusing," Sanders said. "Have you thought of going into musical comedy?"

"No," Ray said thoughtfully, "but I did think of going in to see Eileen's doctor. He told me a lot. Everything, in fact."

Sanders turned, slowly, and his face looked interested for the first time since Ray had stepped into the room.

"Really?" There was a slight waver to his voice.

"Really," Ray said. "I began wondering why she'd see you right after seeing her doctor. I told Dr. Simms I was her brother. He told me all about her, everything I wanted to know." Ray took a deep breath. "Even who the father of the child was."

He waited while his lie registered on Sanders. The color seemed to drain from Sanders's face. He leaned back against the bar, his knuckles whitening with his grip.

"Tony Sanders," Ray said. "Eileen told the doctor all about it."

Sanders turned his back, poured another jigger of Scotch and swallowed it quickly. When he turned to face Ray again, he had regained all his composure.

"So what?" he asked. "What does it mean? Nothing. Not a damned thing."

"It can mean a lot."

"It can mean that a high-grade piece just wasn't very careful."

"It can mean murder," Ray said softly.

"Really, friend, that's absurd. The girl was married and certainly old enough to know what she was doing. I'd hardly kill her for having become pregnant. In fact, I should think the reverse would apply."

"I don't get you."

"You're a little slow on the uptake."

"Sometimes." Ray grinned. "Some people are even slower, though. For example, I never even thought to ask Eileen's doctor who the father was." Ray shrugged. "Maybe he knew. I sure as hell didn't until you told me a few seconds ago."

Sanders's face turned white. He kept his teeth clamped together in a frozen smile, but his eyes were hard and mirthless.

"Get the hell out of here," Sanders said.

"Sure. I was going anyway. I think the police might want to hear about this. It might interest them."

Sanders gave a short, brittle laugh. "You think they'll believe you—take your word over mine?"

Ray considered this for a moment. He studied Sanders's handsome, arrogant face, the expensive cut of his clothes. Sanders, the playboy supreme. His own yacht, and his own plane. He knew the Continent like the back of his hand, had been all over the world— Canada, Mexico, Alaska, India. He was rich, and charming, and poised.

And Ray Stone? One word took care of that as far as the police were concerned. Hophead.

"Maybe you're right," Ray said. "Maybe I'll plow through it myself, Sanders." His voice lowered. "I'm getting closer, lots closer. I haven't got it all yet, but I'm getting pretty damned close. Maybe I'll be back."

"Maybe you won't," Sanders replied.

"We'll see." Ray opened the door and stepped out into the

hallway. He waited outside the door, thinking for a moment, then started down the steps.

He ran down quickly, not sure what his next move would be, but filled with a sense of accomplishment, and feeling better than he had since he'd discovered Eileen's cold body. He was on the last few steps when the lobby door swung open, and a heavily built man walked in.

He sensed Ray's presence, lifted his bent head to look up into his face.

Ray's pulse quickened, and his fingers tightened involuntarily on the banister.

He remembered the deserted farmhouse in Connecticut, and the devastating power of the .45 that had lashed into his face. The muscles alongside his mouth quivered with silent rage mixed with fear.

Through tight lips, he whispered, "Hello, Hank."

## Chapter Eighteen

Hank's brows pulled together, and puzzlement clouded his brown, heavily lidded eyes. Then recognition crossed his face with the delicate slowness of a skulking cat. A grin tilted the corners of his mouth, ludicrously awry beneath his twisted nose.

"If it ain't the junkie," he said.

He stood at the bottom of the steps, looking up at Ray, his long arms hanging at his sides, his fingers widespread and loose. Ray stood on the third step, his eyes alert, one hand still clutching the banister.

"Visiting?" Ray asked.

Hank didn't answer. His eyes raked over the bruises on Ray's face. "You don't look half bad," he said, "considering."

"You tried," Ray said, his voice humorless. "You sure as hell tried."

"Yeah," Hank said dryly. His eyes blinked, and Ray saw the sudden flick of his wrist as his hand started up toward the holster under his left armpit. Warning screamed inside Ray's head. He tensed himself and leaped off the steps.

He clamped his fingers around Hank's right wrist as the .45 swung free of the holster. They stood body to body now, Hank's hand tight around the grip of the .45, Ray's fingers tight around the gun wrist. Hank swung his hand high over his head, trying to shake the fingers off. The fingers wouldn't budge. Ray clung tenaciously, remembering the metallic bite of the .45, knowing too that it carried another bite, a bite that could put holes in a man's head.

They danced backward in a grotesque embrace, Hank swinging

his arm wildly, Ray clinging to the wrist, keeping the gun pointed away from him. With a sickening thud, they slammed into the door. Hank braced himself and shoved, and Ray felt his fingers slide off the wrist. He clutched at skin, pulled at the cuff of Hank's jacket, but his grip was gone. He saw the deadly muzzle of the gun level off and point at his stomach.

Hank grinned, and his breath came rushing out of his mouth in heavy gasps.

"Well— Looks like—you didn't—learn—last time," he said.

Ray didn't answer. He kept his eyes on the gun.

"We'll have to—do a better job—this time."

He moved closer, and Ray realized with sudden clarity that he had to make his play now or never. He swung out with his right hand, smashing his balled fist against the inside of Hank's wrist. His left hand went back simultaneously, uncocked almost instantly with a vicious forward blow.

His fist caught Hank just below the shoulder, spinning him back against the wall. The gun hand swung around as Ray brought his knee up into Hank's groin.

Hank screamed in pain, and his fingers opened wide as he grabbed for his crotch. The .45 clattered to the floor, and Ray made a leap for it, clasping it tightly in a sweating hand.

He gestured impatiently with the gun. "Get up. Come on, get up."

Hank was doubled over in pain, his face a ghastly white. "You son of a bitch," he said.

"Get up!" Ray shouted. "Get up or I'll put a hole in your head."

There was something in his voice that Hank recognized. He staggered to his feet, one hand pressed tight against his stomach.

"Move," Ray said. "The back of the hall. Hurry up."

He gestured with the gun, and Hank moved past the stairwell toward the far end of the lobby.

"Behind the stairs," Ray said.

"Listen, pal—"

"Don't pal *me*, you bastard. Get behind those stairs. We're going to have a little chat."

Hank stood up, his back against the wall. The stairway angled down overhead. Hank's face had lost all its color. His lips trembled a little as he stared at the .45.

"Look, pal, let's—let's just—"

"Let's nothing! Let's shut up and listen. This time I'm asking the questions, Hank-boy, and the answers better be the right ones."

"Now look—"

"What's Sanders got to do with all this?"

"Who's Sanders?"

Ray's eyes snapped with anger. "Look, you bastard, I want straight answers. I know how to use this gun, either end."

"I don't know any Sanders," Hank said.

"What are you doing in this building?"

"Nothing. It's windy outside. I stopped in the lobby to light a cigarette."

Ray flipped the .45 to his left hand, cocked his right fist and brought it across his body in a blow that caught Hank on the side of his cheek.

"Let's hear the story," he whispered.

"There ain't no story," Hank insisted.

Ray's voice was so low it was almost inaudible. "You want to die, don't you? You want to die with a hole in your head."

"If there's nothing to tell, how can I—"

Ray jammed the muzzle of the .45 into Hank's navel. Hank backed tighter against the wall, his face screwing up in pain.

"I'm sore," Ray shouted, his face close to Hank's. "I'm good and sore. I've never been so sore in all my life. I've been chased by every son of a bitch in New York for the past three days. It's getting me, Hank. It's beginning to eat at me like a cancer. If you don't start talking soon, I'm going to split wide open. I'm going to squeeze the trigger of this cannon, and I'm going to keep squeezing until it's empty. They'll scrape you off the wall, you son of a bitch, and it won't bother me one bit. I can still remember Connecticut, Hank, I can remember it fine, and the more I remember it, and the more you stall, the sorer I get. I'm getting so sore that I'm liable to ram this gun clear through you, squeezing the trigger all the way. You understand, Hank? You understand?"

"Look, Stone, take it—"

"I don't want to hear wasted talk, Hank. If you talk, you say something. I'm not interested in anything else."

"Well—"

Ray's voice was tight and strained. He struggled to keep it from shaking, but the trembling was all through his body now and the gun was hot and heavy in his hand, "Hank, I'm not kidding, Hank. I'm going to put a tunnel in you in about three—"

"All right," Hank said. A fine sheen of sweat was on his forehead, and fear was etched plainly against his ashen features.

"I'm listening."

"I was coming to see Sanders."

"Why?"

"He—he's still looking for the stuff."

"Don't lie to me, Hank."

"That's the truth, so help me."

"Did he have me beat up?"

"Yes."

"How did he know where to find me? How'd you know where to look?"

"I don't know."

"Hank—"

"I don't know. He told me you'd be on Seventy-third. That's where we looked. That's where we found you."

"All right. All right." Ray's mind was working frantically. The pieces were falling together now, fitting snugly. He backed away from Hank, his eyes narrowed, his mouth thin. With one sudden movement, he brought the .45 up in a swinging arc, the metal colliding against the side of Hank's head. Hank looked surprised for an instant, and then his eyes went blank and he flopped against the wall, sliding gently to the floor.

Ray ran to the stairway and took the steps up two at a time. He stopped outside Sanders's door, rapped on it with the muzzle of the big gun. The door opened a crack and Ray shoved it all the way open, the .45 out in front of him. Sanders looked at the gun; then his eyes wandered up to meet Ray's.

"Expecting someone else, weren't you?" Ray asked. His back was against the door, and he kept the .45 trained on Sanders's stomach.

"No, I—"

"He's downstairs, behind the staircase. He's got a big lump on the side of his head. I put it there."

"Look, friend, I don't know what you're—"

"You can drop the 'friend' routine," Ray snapped.

"All right, Stone, what's on your mind?"

"A lot of things, Sanders. And they all stink. I told you I was close. Well, I'm not close any more. I'm there. It's all here inside my head, Sanders. All the facts. They add up to you."

"Are you still harping on your pet theory? Do you still think I killed—"

"I don't think it, I know it. There was one thing that threw me, but that's all figured out now."

"That's fine," Sanders said. A bored look had come onto his face again. He looked at Ray with mild disinterest.

"Tony Sanders, millionaire playboy. Always hopping off to another corner of the world. The hundred-percent American traveler abroad. Sure, very sweet. A very sweet setup."

"Nothing wrong with traveling, Stone."

"Nothing at all. Unless you pick up odds and ends of narcotics on your little trips. Then it becomes a crime."

"Another of your theories, Stone?"

"I've got more, Sanders. Just lend an ear. It was hard to tie up Massine's death with Eileen's, until your boyfriend downstairs told me who'd ordered my beating. I knew who wanted the heroin then, and it was pretty simple to figure that you were the boy who was importing the stuff. But it wouldn't do to have Tony Sanders pushing the junk. Hell, no. Sanders is a respected citizen with a lust for travel. Sanders couldn't push it. But Massine could. Massine could keep your lily-white hands clean."

Sanders reached over to the cigarette box, lifted the lid, seemed to discover it empty. Ray watched him as he crossed the room in search of a cigarette.

"All right," Ray said, "Massine was pushing it for you. The supplier and the pusher, a very neat setup. And the best part was that no one would ever suspect a tie-up."

"That's quite possible," Sanders said, reaching for a second cigarette box on top of one of the low bookcases. "In fact, you've just about hit the nail on the head."

"I've got more, Sanders. Funny how it all fell into place all of a sudden. I should have known from the very—"

He saw Sanders's arm whip back, saw the heavy metal cigarette box arc across the room. He tried to dodge it, but he was too late, and Sanders had already thrown his heavy body into a forward tackle. The box slammed against his hand, and almost immediately afterward, he felt Sanders's arms tighten around his knees. He tried to keep his balance against the momentum of Sanders's flying leap, but felt his knees give.

Sanders was pounding Ray's gun hand against the floor with savage intensity. He tried to struggle free, but Sanders's grip was a strong one. Ray felt the gun slipping from his grasp, and suddenly Sanders was standing over him with the gun pointed down at his head.

"Let's hear the rest of your story, Stone. I'm curious. It doesn't matter because I'm going to shoot you and then call the police. But I'm curious."

"You'd never get away with it. You think another murder will help you?"

"This will be my first murder, Stone. I didn't kill Eileen or Charlie, and I rather resent your insisting on it."

"Hank then. What's the difference? You ordered both killings. It's the same thing."

"I think we can stop playing with each other, Stone. I know you killed Eileen, and I know you stole that tin of heroin. We've been waiting for you to lead us to it." He grinned crookedly. "You've got a strong constitution."

"You were buying the stuff then? On your trips?"

"Sure. Mexico, Italy, Spain, France. Who suspects a playboy? Playboys are supposed to be fun-loving dolts, not businessmen."

"And Charlie was pushing it for you?"

"Of course."

"Then why'd you kill him?"

"Don't say that again, Stone," Sanders warned.

"You shot Eileen to get back the heroin she'd stolen from you, isn't that it?"

"You're guessing, Stone."

"Sure, I'm guessing. Eileen came up to see you after she visited the doctor. She found something she hadn't bargained for, though. Sixteen ounces of pure heroin done up in a candy tin. She swiped it and later you discovered it and came after her."

"I didn't know the heroin was missing until I read of Eileen's death in the papers," Sanders said.

"You killed her," Ray insisted. "You took the horse and pumped the slugs into her belly. You left me for the patsy."

It felt wrong. He knew it was wrong even as he said it, but he went on anyway. Something was missing. Something big. He didn't know what, though, and so he kept talking.

"After you killed Eileen, you realized that Charlie would know immediately who'd done it. Charlie was in on the whole setup, and he'd know you killed her for the heroin."

*But Charlie had been surprised when Ray told him about the sixteen ounces. Something was wrong. Damn it, something was wrong.*

"So you had to kill Charlie too, just to make sure you'd be safe."

*But why would he? Charlie was his partner, his pusher. Without Charlie, Sanders would have been helpless. Besides, why should Charlie care about the death of a junkie?*

"You've got a wonderful imagination," Sanders said. "You're wrong, though. Dead wrong."

He knew. He knew he was wrong, but he didn't know where. *Charlie.* How could Sanders have killed Charlie when—

Ray shook his head. He had to get out of here. Fast.

"What are you going to do with me?" he asked.

"I'm going to put one hole in the middle of your forehead. I'm then going to call the police and tell them I've got the murderer. I'll tell them you threatened me with a gun, that I disarmed you, and was forced to shoot you."

Ray's eyes shifted to the gun. *A chance. A slim chance.* He began chuckling, softly at first, and then a little louder. The chuckling came hard because his stomach was tied into knots, and he certainly didn't feel like laughing. Still, it might work, it just might work.

"You expect to shoot me with that gun?" he asked. He was laughing out loud now. He sat at Sanders's feet, and Sanders looked down at him in puzzlement.

"It's not loaded," he roared. "The damned thing is empty!"

There was just an instant of indecision, a bare instant during which Sanders took his eyes from Ray and shifted them to the gun. The gun came up a fraction of an inch, moving away from Ray. Sanders realized it was a trick then, but he was too late. Ray kicked out with his heel, felt the smack of his shoe against Sanders's shin. He leaped to his feet. His fist lashed out with all the power of his arm and shoulder behind it.

Sanders was reaching for his shin when Ray's fist collided with the point of his jaw. He straightened abruptly as the shock of contact raced up Ray's arm, singing into his shoulder.

Sanders's eyes glazed. He folded gently, the .45 dropping from his lax fingers. He was slow falling, and Ray slugged him again, catching him under the jaw as he toppled forward.

He collapsed like a wet rag, his eyes wide and glassy.

Ray understood it all now, every bit of it. It was simple. He should have known it all along because it had stared him right in the face for a long time.

He left quickly.

# Chapter Nineteen

Ray wondered if he were too late. Perhaps the apartment was empty. He stood outside the door and pressed the push button, rattling the knob with his other hand.

"Open up," he shouted.

"Just a minute."

He waited patiently, his heart loud in his ears. The peephole didn't open, and he surmised that his voice had been recognized.

The door swung wide, and he caught his breath at the sight of her.

Her black hair was swept to one side of her head, leaving a free, sweeping line on the other side, exposing the flawless curve of her face and neck. Her lips were heavily rouged, parted to show white teeth. Her lashes were dark and sooty around her eyes; the hollow of her throat deep.

She wore white.

The gown was skin-tight, following every line of her body, sweeping over her wide hips, hugging her thighs.

"You're back," she said. Her voice was cold, distant.

"Yes, Babs, I'm back."

"Come in." It was not an invitation. It was resignation to an inescapable fact. He stepped into the apartment and she closed the door gently behind him. "You're wasting your time, Ray," she said. "It's all over."

"I know," he said softly. "That's why I'm here."

"To pick up the pieces?"

"Something like that. Yes, to pick up the pieces."

"There's nothing to pick up." She speared a cigarette from a container on the coffee table, put it between her lips. He leaned over for the silver lighter and put flame to it.

"Thanks," she said.

"You're a funny gal," he said, putting the lighter back on the table.

"Ray, I haven't got time for idle talk. I'm due at the club by nine."

"The club can wait," he said harshly.

"If you came here to make a scene, I—"

"I came here to make a scene, Babs. I came here to make a damned big scene."

"We're finished, Ray. Over and done with. I don't like to share my men, especially with Chinese sluts who—"

"I know. I should have had the answer when you went into your jealous fit a little while back."

"Stop talking riddles." She blew out smoke in a furious stream, cupped her elbow in her other hand.

"You liked Sanders, didn't you?"

Babs stared at him silently, a crafty look coming into her eyes. "What's this all about?" she asked.

"It's about the murder of Eileen Chalmers."

"Oh."

"That's all? Just a small oh?"

"What do you want me to say? The girl is dead."

"Sure. And you killed her."

"What?" Babs snorted contemptuously. "Are you out of your mind?"

"I was, Babs. No more now, though. I'm thinking straight for the first time in three days."

"Why would I kill Eileen? She was my friend." She drew in on the cigarette again. "This is absurd, Ray."

"Not so absurd. Eileen was your friend, true. But Sanders was your business partner."

"Business?" A surprised look crossed her face, leaving her brows high on her forehead. "Really, Ray—"

"It took me a while to figure it. You, Sanders, and Massine. The triumvirate. Sanders picked up the stuff on his little jaunts, and you and Massine distributed it. It was really simple. When the Kramer band went on the road, Charlie pushed the stuff. You did the same thing with the Lewis combo, all over the country. Nationwide distribution. A wonderful setup."

"What stuff are you referring to?"

"Cut it, Babs. I'm on to you, don't you see? I know all about it now, so we can stop kidding each other."

"I still don't know what you're talking about."

"All right," Ray said tiredly. "We'll do it the hard way. I'll explain it. I'll explain it all. Then you'll know I'm not bluffing. Then we can call the police."

"You'd better explain," she said. She put out her cigarette, lighted another one.

"The heroin. Sanders supplied, you and Charlie distributed. That was fine—until you decided you wanted more from Sanders than a simple business partner. You wanted Sanders, period. That might have worked, too. He liked you and he dated you, and he probably slept with you."

"You're getting insulting," Babs said.

"Still playing the great lady. You didn't feel so ladylike when you found out Sanders was seeing Eileen, did you? I can imagine the jealous fit you threw when you learned about her coming baby. That must have really given you a laugh. It was so amusing that you decided to kill Eileen, get her out of the way so that you'd have a clear path with Sanders. No second fiddle for Barbara Cole. All or nothing at all."

Babs was silent now. She puffed meditatively on her cigarette, watching Ray as he spoke.

"I should have tumbled when I saw this place. Your clothes, the whole layout, all smelled of money. More money than any band vocalist ever made. But narcotics is a lucrative business. That should have tipped me. It didn't. I'm slow, I guess. I didn't catch on.

"And then you gave me another tip, a tip that should have blown the whole thing sky-high. But I was considering a few nice things you did that morning, and the full meaning didn't hit me."

"What are you talking about?"

"Your note. A full band rehearsal, you said. You said you had to be there. The first time I met Kramer, he was having a rehearsal. I asked him where his vocalist was, and he told me she never rehearsed with the band. It didn't click when I read your note. I was too busy concentrating on the last part of it, the part that asked me to wait for you, the part that said you'd have something for me. You probably meant your body, and you were right in thinking I'd wait around for that. It could have meant heroin, though I doubt if you planned it that way, and I'd sure as hell wait for that, too. Either way, you wanted to make sure I'd be there when the cops arrived. That's why you pressed my suit, or had it pressed, and washed my shirt. You were putting me in a nice frame of mind, to make sure I'd stay there and get nabbed by the cops."

"That's silly. I could have turned you in at any time. Why should I have sneaked around about it?"

"That puzzled me, too. I wondered why you hadn't turned me in before. But then I realized that the cops showed up only *after* I told you I thought Eileen had been killed for the heroin. You knew then that I knew about the missing horse. Before that you weren't sure.

"You see, I kept wondering why anyone would bother to kill Eileen. If they wanted the heroin, all they had to do was take it. Eileen and I were both higher than the moon. I figured then that whoever'd killed her had wanted her dead besides wanting the heroin. I thought this was Sanders until just a little while ago. He had every reason to kill her, being the father of her unborn child, and wanting to get her out of his hair. But Sanders didn't know the horse was gone until he read about it in the papers. If he'd killed Eileen and lifted the heroin, he wouldn't have had me beaten to find out where it was.

"The way I figure it now, the heroin was just an accident. You came up to Eileen's room with the express purpose of killing her. You couldn't have known that she'd stolen the stuff from Sanders that afternoon. But when you found it there, you picked it up, and that gave you more ideas."

Babs turned her back to Ray, walked over to a cabinet against the wall and leaned on it, facing him again.

"Oh, I know you killed Eileen, Babs. You killed Massine, too. It had to be you. In the beginning, Massine was the only person I told about the sixteen ounces, and he was surprised as hell. When I left him, I called you about half an hour later. You weren't home. I went to see Sanders then, and when I went back to Massine, he was dead. Sanders couldn't have done it. Massine had contacted someone else, someone he could tell his startling information to. That someone was you. I knew it wasn't Sanders because I was with him all the while. Does that make sense?"

"Why should I kill Massine if what you say is true? What possible purpose would that serve?"

"Simple. This is where your bigger ideas come in. You had sixteen ounces of heroin now—pure heroin, worth a fortune. Sanders didn't know you had it, and Massine didn't know, either. With Eileen out of the way, you had smooth sailing from there on in with Sanders. But why split the take three ways? You'd switched to Kramer's band when the Lewis combo got stalled down in the Ace High. You sure as hell couldn't distribute on a band that stayed in one place. Eileen was happy to make the change; anything to get away from her husband. All right, there were now two of you on Kramer's band, you and Massine. Why take Massine into the picture at all? When he told you he knew about the sixteen ounces, you probably told him to stay right where he was, that you'd be right over. You went over, all right, and you put a hole between his eyes."

Babs smiled. She turned and opened a drawer in the cabinet. When she faced him again, she was holding a Luger in her hand. A silencer was attached to the muzzle of the gun. He looked at the weapon uncomprehendingly for a moment. He had not suspected he was so close to goading her into action, and yet he was not really surprised by the gun because she had turned and lifted it from the drawer as casually as if she were reaching for silverware.

"Is that the gun you used?" he asked.

"Yes," she said. Quickly, she slid out the clip. She put the clip on the cabinet behind her and then she held out the gun to Ray. "Here," she said, "take it."

He took the Luger, puzzled. She was back at the cabinet again, opening another drawer, and then turning once more. This time she was holding a candy tin on her open palm, the same tin Eileen had showed him three nights ago in the hotel. His pulse quickened at the sight of it.

"I was right, then," he said.

"Except about one thing. If I'd planned to share this with Sanders, why didn't I tell him about it?"

He thought this over, his forehead creasing. "Maybe you planned to cross him, too. How should I know?"

Babs's lashes lowered, and a sensuous look crossed her face. "You came along, Ray. You came along, and I didn't want to share this with anyone but you. That's why I didn't tell Sanders I had it. That's why I let him go on his own wild-goose chase searching for it."

"Bull!" Ray shouted. "If you cared so much about me, why'd you tell Sanders where his goons could pick me up? That was another tipoff, Babs. I called you just before I went to see Eileen's doctor. You were the only one who knew where I was. And then suddenly I'm picked up and worked over. Funny how you don't think of these things at the time. You're too caught up in the present. I was too busy getting my brains beat out."

"I had to do that, Ray," she said. She had reached into the drawer again, her back to him, and he saw the glint of a metallic object as she placed it on top of the cabinet. "If I hadn't told Tony where to find you, he'd have suspected me. That would have ruined all my plans. All my plans for you and me, darling."

"You didn't have to tell him anything, Babs. He didn't know I'd called you."

"He was here when you phoned."

"Pretty damned convenient, all right."

"He was here because he was worried about the loss of the heroin. Do you realize how much that tin is worth, Ray? We'll be rich! Just you and me. There's enough here to set us up for life."

Ray thought of the heroin again, and a shiver ran up his spine. It had been three days, and there were sixteen ounces across the room on the cabinet. What the hell was she doing there, he wondered. Why didn't she face him?

"Besides, Ray," she said softly, turning her head over her shoulder, "I didn't know he would hurt you. Tony was always gentle. I didn't know he'd call in any outsiders. I didn't want you hurt then, and I don't want you hurt now. If I planned to hurt you, would I have given you my gun? Would I be talking to you like—"

"You can save it, Babs," he said. "You're a murderer, and I'm calling the police."

She turned then, and he realized what she'd been doing at the cabinet. She was cooking a fix. Christ, it had been long, too long. Ray stared at the heroin in fascination, the blood rushing through his veins.

She reached into the open drawer again. When she withdrew her hand, she was holding a hypodermic. Carefully, gingerly, she put the spoon down on the cabinet top.

"Just a little while longer, Ray," she said. "Just a little while. I'm going to fix you, honey. I'm going to give you the ride you've been dying for. Just a little while, honey."

He didn't say a word. He watched her as she expertly sucked the heroin into the syringe. He saw the white fluid filling the glass cylinder, and he wet his lips. A white-hot flame was licking at his chest now, searing his stomach.

Heroin, heroin. The old song sang in his ears beneath the steady beat of his blood. Heroin, heroin!

There was a fix across the room, waiting. After all this time, there was a fix.

She turned away from the cabinet again, held the needle up to the light. Then she faced him fully, smiling at him, holding the loaded hypo in her right hand.

He looked at her, his heart beating rapidly. His eyes followed the taper of her arm to the hypo she held in her hand. The needle tip caught little flecks of light, snapped them back into the room.

"You and me," she said huskily, "and a fortune in heroin, Ray. Just you and me."

She was closer to him now. She held the needle poised in her right hand, and she was breathing heavily.

"You can have both, Ray, in any order you want them. Me, and the heroin in this syringe."

He looked at the hypo again, wet his lips. Babs and the heroin, both.

She held the needle out and whispered, "Take it, Ray, Take it. Take it. You need it, Ray. Go on, take it."

There was something in the voice that irritated him. He'd heard the voice before. It belonged to Phil Ragow, and to Louis, and to Charlie Massine. It belonged to every pusher he'd ever known, the oily coaxing, the gentle insistence, the almost pleading quality.

"Go on, Ray," she said, and her voice was soft. "Take the needle."

He looked at the needle. He thought of all the other needles he'd ever had, and the sweat broke out on his brow, covered the back of his hands, ran down his back. Three days it had been, three whole days without a shot. How long could you go without a fix? How long could you go before you dropped dead?

"Do you want me first, Ray? Is that it, baby? Me first, and then the shot. All right, baby. Any way you say. Anything you want."

But he hadn't died. He hadn't dropped dead. It had been three days without a fix, and he was still alive. Why not another three days? Did it get worse? How much worse could it get? If he had help. Jeannie. Maybe Jeannie.

"No!" he shouted. "I don't want it!"

Babs stared at him incredulously. "What?"

"I don't want it. Neither, neither of you. You or the heroin. I'm calling the police, Babs. I don't want it, do you understand?"

He was bellowing now, trying to convince himself as well as Babs. "I don't want it. God damn it, I don't want it!"

Her eyes narrowed against the whiteness of her face. Her skin seemed to have stretched tight over her cheekbones, and her lips skinned back over her teeth.

"I'm not asking anymore, Ray. You're taking it whether you want it or not!"

Her face was an ugly thing as she came slowly forward, the needle poised for a strike, her thumb on the plunger. He wondered how he could have thought she was beautiful, wondered how he could have found anything in her to love. He watched the needle approach him, and he suddenly caught at her arm, swinging her around sharply. Her head snapped back and she dropped the needle. She scrabbled for it on the rug, and he kicked it away with his foot. She crouched on the floor, her eyes flaming hatred, her breast heaving, her nails digging into the carpet.

"You cheap hophead," she screamed. "You lousy cheap bastard!"

All the revulsion he felt for her welled up into his throat. All the horror and degradation of the drug choked him, clouded his eyes with blind rage. He reached down and yanked her to her feet. He looked at her for a brief instant as she kept screaming at him, and then he drove his fist into her face, hard, feeling the bones yield to his knuckles. It was the first time he'd ever hit a woman.

She collapsed to the floor and he stood over her, panting. Beside her on the floor lay the hypodermic.

He reached down for it, and his fingers responded to the familiar grip of the tube. His eyes wandered over the heroin, opened in surprise as he read the markings inside the tube.

There was enough heroin inside that glass cylinder to kill a bull! Far more than the two grains that made up a lethal dose.

She was going to fix him, all right. This was to be the big fix, and there would never have been another one for Ray. He looked at the cylinder again, and a smile crossed his face.

He dropped the hypo to the rug, smashed it beneath his heel. The heroin made a large blot on the rug, spreading beneath his shoe.

He stared at the shattered syringe, then walked to the phone and dialed the operator.

"Give me the police," he said.

# WANT MORE
# McBAIN?

Read on for a
long-lost novelette by
**ED McBAIN**
featuring MATT CORDELL,
the disgraced detective from
THE GUTTER AND THE GRAVE.

And for another exciting
novel-length crime story,
THE GUTTER AND THE GRAVE
is available now from your favorite
local or online bookseller!

## Die Hard

The bar was the kind of dimly lit outhouse you find in any run-down neighborhood, except that it was a little more ragged around the edges. There were blue and white streamers crowding the ceiling, arranged in a criss-cross pattern strung up in celebration of some local hero's return a long time ago. The mirror behind the bar was cracked, and it lifted one half of my face higher than the other. A little to the right of the bar was a door with a sign that cutely said, *Little Boys.* The odor seeping through the woodwork wasn't half as cute.

A few stumblebums were spilled over the tables in the joint like a troupe of marionettes with cut strings. I was the only guy standing besides the bartender, and if events followed their customary pattern, I wouldn't be standing long. That's the beauty of a perpetual bender. You know just when you've had all that you can hold, and you go on from there.

I lifted the shot glass from the bar, and went on from there. When I put the glass down, he was standing by my elbow, a hopeful expression on his face. "Mr. Cordell?" he asked.

He was a little man with a little voice, one of the many stamped from the mold, one of those subway-strappers. He had a round face with a long nose that tried its damnedest to peer into his mouth. His lips were thin and narrow, and his eyes were carrying luggage, heavy luggage.

"Yeah," I said, "I'm Cordell."

He hesitated, looking over his shoulder, and then fastened two pale blue eyes on my face. "I...I understand you're a private detective," he said.

I turned my back to him and studied the empty shot glass. "You understand wrong, mister," I said.

"I need help," he went on, "for my son. My son."

"I'm not a detective," I told him, my voice rising slightly. I signaled for the bartender, and he nodded at me from the other end of the bar. The small man moved closer to me.

"My son," he said. "He's an addict."

"That's too bad," I told him, my voice tired.

"I want you to stop them, the ones who made him that way, the ones who keep giving him that…that…filth!"

"You're asking me to stop the tide, mister," I said. "I couldn't do that if I wanted to. And I don't want to. Leave me alone, will you?"

"Please," he said. "I…"

"Look, mister, I'm not interested. Shove off. Blow."

His eyes slitted, and for just one moment the small man became a big man, an outraged man. "What kind of person are you, anyway?" he asked. His voice was thin and tight. "I need your help. I come to you for help. I need you, do you understand?"

The effort seemed to weaken him. He slumped against the bar, pulling a soiled handkerchief from his hip pocket and wiping it across his forehead.

"I can't help you," I said, my voice a little gentler. I was wondering what the hell was keeping the bartender. "I'm not a private detective anymore. My license has been revoked, understand? I can't practice in this state anymore."

He stared at me, his head making little nodding movements. When I'd finished speaking, he said, "My son doesn't know about licenses. He knows only the needle. To take the needle away, you don't need a fancy piece of paper."

"No," I agreed. "You need a hell of a lot more than that."

"You'll help me then?"

"No!"

He seemed astonished. He opened his hands and his eyes simultaneously and asked, "But why? Why not? Why can't…"

I banged my glass on the bar and yelled, "Hey, bartender, what the hell are you doing, fermenting it?" I turned to face the little man fully then, and my voice was very low when I spoke. "Mister," I said, "you're wasting your time. I'm not interested, don't you see? Not in your son, or anybody's son. Not even in my own mother's son. Please understand and just leave me alone. Go back to your nice little apartment and get the hell out of this cruddy dive. Just go. Do me a favor. Go."

All color drained out of his face. His head pulled in like a turtle's and he murmured, "It's no use, then. No use." He turned and headed for the door just as the bartender ambled over.

"Give me another of the same," I said. I didn't watch the little man leave. I watched the bartender instead, and I watched the way the whisky spilled from the neck of the bottle over the lip of the glass.

The pistol shots were rapid and short. Two in a row. Two short cracks like the beat of a stick against a snare drum rim. I lifted my head and turned it toward the door just in time to see the small man reach out for the door jamb. He fell against his own hand and began dropping toward the floor slowly, like a blob of butter sliding down a knife. A streak of crimson followed his body down the length of the jamb, and then he collapsed on the floor in a lifeless little ball.

I ran over to the door and threw it wide. The street outside was dark, covered with a filmy rain slick, dimly lighted by a solitary lamppost on the corner. I could hear the staccato click of heels running against asphalt, dying out against the blackness of the city.

I turned back to the small man. The bartender was already leaning over him. "You know him?" he asked.

"No."

"Looks to me like you knew him."

I reached up and grabbed the front of the bartender's shirt, twisting it in my fist. "I said I don't know him. Just remember that. When the cops crawl out of the woodwork, just remember I never saw this guy in my life." I pulled his face down to mine. "Remember?"

"I'll remember," he said.

"Good. Go mix a Pink Lady or something." I shoved him away from me and he walked back to the bar, a sulky look on his face.

I felt for a pulse, knowing damn well I wouldn't find one. I took out the small man's wallet then, and found a driver's license made out to Peter D'Allessio. I memorized his address, then put the license back into the wallet. I turned the plastic leaves, saw several pictures of a nice-looking kid with a prominent nose and light-colored eyes. D'Allessio's son, I figured. The addict. He didn't look like an addict. He had a full face and a big smile spread over it. His teeth were strong and even. I snapped the wallet shut and put it back into D'Allessio's pocket, even though he wouldn't be needing anything in that wallet again.

I passed the bartender and went straight to the phone. I dropped a dime in and then dialed the big O for Operator.

"Your call, please," she said in a crisp voice.

"Give me the police."

"Do you wish to report a crime?"

"No, a strawberry festival."

"What?"

"For Pete's sake, get me the police."

I sat in the booth until a tired voice said, "Twelfth Precinct, Cassidy."

"I want to report a murder."

His voice got businesslike. "Where?"

I told him.

"Did you witness it?"

"No. I saw the guy die, but I didn't see who did it."

"May I have your name, sir?"

"No," I said, and hung up.

That was that. My hands were washed. I left the booth and walked straight out of the bar, not looking down at D'Allessio. It was dark in the street, and I hesitated for a moment, wondering where to go now, wondering what to do next. Another bar? Sure, why not? I started walking, and I could hear the moan of the police sirens in the distance as they closed in on the remains of a little man who'd had a big problem.

She found me at my hotel the next morning. I was lying there with the sheet pulled over my face when the knock sounded on the door.

"Who is it?" I called, the effort starting the little hammers going inside my head. I tried sitting up.

"You don't know me."

"What do you want, then?"

"I want to talk to you."

I shrugged and called, "It should be open. Walk in." She stepped into the room, closing the door behind her. She was small and dark, with her hair pulled tight against the side of her face and caught in a ponytail at the back of her neck. Her face was a narrow oval that framed deep brown eyes and a straight nose. Her lips were well shaped. She wore a white blouse open at the throat, revealing the firm, subtle rise of the young breasts that filled out the blouse.

"Mr. Cordell?" she asked.

"What do you want?"

"I want to talk to you about Jerry D'Allessio."

"Oh, nuts."

"Did I say something wrong?"

"Sister, call off the hounds. First the old man and now…"

She moved across the room and stopped near the bed. "Was Mr. D'Allessio…did he contact you, too?"

"He did. He did that."

"He's dead. You know he's dead?"

"I know."

"They did it, Mr. Cordell. They knew he was trying to do something about Jerry. They wanted to shut him up."

"They shut him up fine," I said. I rubbed a hand over the bristle on my chin. "Listen, who's giving me free publicity? Who's parking you people on my doorstep? I'm curious."

Her eyes were serious when she answered, "Everybody knows about you, Mr. Cordell."

"Then you also know I'm no longer practicing. I'm out of business. We held the clearance sale a long while back."

"You're talking about your wife, aren't you?"

It startled me. It startled the hell out of me because she said it so calmly and because it split a raw wound wide open.

"I think you'd better get the hell out of here," I said.

"It's no secret, so there's nothing to hide," she went on. "It was in all the papers."

"Are you leaving or do you get kicked out on your can?"

Her eyes leveled on mine, and she said, "Don't play it hard, Cordell. I don't scare."

"Look…"

"So your wife was playing around," she said sharply. "So what? You should live in our neighborhood. The wives who *don't* play around are either crippled or dead."

"I don't want to talk about it," I said. I was beginning to tense up. I was beginning to want to smash things.

"He deserved everything you gave him," she said. "He deserved the beating."

"Thanks. The police didn't quite see it your way."

"You shouldn't have used the end of a forty-five. You should have…"

"Little girl," I said, "blow. I don't like rehashing dead cases."

"*You* died with the case, brave man," she said. "You died when they snatched your license."

"Listen…"

"What'd you expect? A gold star?" She was standing close to the bed now, her lips skinned back. "What makes a private eye think he's got rights an ordinary citizen hasn't? Assault with a deadly weapon, wasn't it?"

"She was a tramp," I blurted, "and he was a punk. I should have killed him. I should have killed the louse. I should have…"

She was taunting me now, her hands on her hips, her chest thrust out. "You couldn't kill a corpse," she said. "You couldn't…"

I lashed out with the open palm of my right hand, catching her on the side of her jaw. The blow knocked her halfway across the room, but she came back like a wildcat, leaping onto the bed, her fingernails raking the length of my arm.

I was sore. I was good and sore. She was something to smash, and she had started it all. She was wriggling and squirming under my grip. She kicked out and her skirt rode up over her thighs, exposing a cool white expanse of flesh. The sheet slid down over my knees and I threw her flat on her back and rammed my lips against hers, hard. My hands fumbled with her blouse and then gradually her lips came alive under mine and she stopped struggling.

She'd brought it all back, every bit of it. She'd brought back the picture of Toni with her blonde hair cascading down her back, her laughing mouth, her deep eyes, green like a jungle glade. Four months of marriage, and then Parker. I should have used the business end on him. I should have squeezed the trigger and kept squeezing until he was just a dirty smear on the rug.

I was trembling with fury now, and I took it out on her. She moaned softly, her arms tight around my neck, yielding to me, her eyes smoky, her lips swollen. She screamed, and the scream was loud in the sun-filtered room. She screamed again and again, and I wanted to scream with her.

And then it was quiet, and she lay back against the pillows, her face flushed, her skirt crumpled around her thighs.

"Will you find Jerry?" she said at last.

"I'll think about it."

"What does that mean?"

"Just what it sounded like. I'll think about it."

"All right." She pulled her skirt down and then stood up, smoothing out her hair. "I'll go. I'll go while you think."

"Sure."

She walked toward the door and turned with her hand on the knob. "Think hard, Cordell," she said.

Then she was gone.

I thought of her and of the fury that had been her body, and she got all mixed up with Toni in my mind. I began to tremble again, the way I always did when I thought of Toni and that night long ago. In my own goddam bedroom, like a two-bit floozie with some bum she'd picked up, his hands roaming over her skin, his mouth buried in her throat, his...

I slammed my fist into the open palm of my other hand.

This was no good. It was over and done with. They'd dropped charges, but the police felt I wasn't worthy of keeping a license.

Where were they now? Mexico for the divorce, and then where? Who cares, I told myself, who cares about it?

I knew who cared.

The guy who bathed every night in enough alcohol to float the *Missouri*. Straight down the gullet, eating a hole in my stomach, but never eating away the scar on my heart.

I rubbed my face with my hand, trying to blot out the memories. The girl hadn't helped. She hadn't helped at all. She'd made it only worse, the way they all did, all of them after Toni. I found a half-dead soldier in the drawer of the nightstand and I poured a stiff one.

I wondered what D'Allessio was addicted to.

Forget it, I said to myself. Who cares?

I took another drink, and I thought of the kid again, and then I took another. And another. Things were getting nice and fuzzy, and a little bit warm. The pain was going away, and I felt a big-brother feeling for a kid I'd never met, a kid who bore a cross just like mine. Except his cross had thorns, and they probably stuck into his arms at four-hour intervals.

I got up and put on my jacket, and I headed for the address that had been on Peter D'Allessio's driver's license.

The address I'd memorized belonged to a gray building that poked at the sky like a blackened finger. A blonde sat on the front stoop, rocking a baby carriage. She looked me over when I started up the steps, her face showing disappointment.

I didn't smile. I knew what I looked like, but I didn't give a damn. She took me in for another minute, her gaze shifting from my bloodshot eyes to the stubble on my chin. Her eyes passed over my rumpled suit, and then she turned back to rocking the carriage with a vengeance.

I lit a match in the hallway and found D'Allessio on a mailbox whose front had been pushed in. *3-B*, the box said. I started up the steps, holding my breath against the stale odors that crawled out of the woodwork.

On the third floor, I stopped in front of 3-B and knocked on the door.

I listened as a pair of bare feet shuffled to the doorway. The

door swung wide, and a thin girl in a faded wrapper stood silhou-
etted against the sunlight that streamed through the window at
the other end of the kitchen.

"Well," she said, "who are *you*?"

"Matt Cordell. Who are you?"

She smiled the oldest smile in the world and said, "What difference does it make? Who sent you up?"

"Where's Jerry D'Allessio?" I asked.

She shrugged. "Hopped to the ears, probably. Who cares?"

"I care. Who *are* you, baby?"

"Let's say I'm his cousin Marie. Why do you want him?"

"Does he live here?"

"Yeah, him and the old man. 'Cept the old man is dead, and
Jerry never comes home. You ain't a cop, are you?" She looked
at me hard. "No, you couldn't be a cop."

"No, I couldn't. Where does Jerry usually hang out?"

"Wherever there's H, you'll find Jerry. Sniff out the hoss,
and you'll find Jerry standing there with his spoon. You could
use a shave, you know."

"I know."

She looked at me again and said, "You might look for Claire
Blaney. Later. She knows Jerry."

"A small, dark girl?"

"Small? Dark? Oh, you're thinking of Edith Rossi. No, I mean
Claire. She's something else."

"How do you mean?"

"Edith and Jerry were engaged."

"Were?"

"Yeah, no more."

"Why not?"

"Were you ever engaged to a junkie, mister? It's no picnic.
Maybe Edith got tired of the things she had to do to get money
for him. Maybe she had it right up to here."

"Why does she want to help him, then?"

For a moment, the hard mask dropped from the girl's face, and there was almost a tenderness about her tired eyes. "She remembers, I guess. She remembers sometimes what Jerry used to be like. I guess that's it."

"Thanks," I said. "Thanks for the information."

"Hey, you leaving?"

"Yep."

"Ain't you stayin' for the ball?"

"What ball?"

"We could build a real ball, mister. Just shave, that's all."

I looked at her, my face expressionless. "Thanks," I said. "The beard keeps me warm."

I left her standing in the doorway, a puzzled look on her face. When I reached the street, I glanced down at the blonde. She didn't look up this time. I walked past her and headed for the nearest candy store. I squeezed up to the counter and ordered an egg cream.

A pimply faced clerk nodded and began mixing it, going very light on the milk. He shoved it across the counter at me and I tasted it. I wasn't used to egg creams.

"What's the matter?" he asked. "No good?"

"Fine," I said. I looked at him hard and added, "The monkey don't like it, that's all."

"Yeah?"

"Yeah. Weighs fifteen pounds, that goddam monkey, and he's scratching away at my shoulder."

"Yeah?"

"I'd sure like to get rid of it," I said, watching his eyes.

"Try the Bronx Zoo," he answered.

"I tried them. They feed their monkey bananas."

The clerk didn't bat an eye. He kept staring at me, and then he said, "There's another zoo in Central Park, mister."

"This monkey, chum, he's scratching hell out of…"

"You're barking up the wrong tree, mister," the clerk said.

"Where's the right tree?"

He blinked once. "Ask your monkey," he said.

He turned his back and walked down to the other end of the counter. When he came back, he had a match stuck between his teeth and he chewed on it as if it were a licorice stick. I tried a new question.

"Where do I find Claire Blaney?"

He looked at me hard, the matchstick unwavering. "You a bull?"

"Don't make me sick."

"The red building on the corner." He studied me again. "You can't miss it. She's on the sixth floor. Blaney. Claire Blaney."

"Thanks," I said.

He nodded. "She ain't gonna help your monkey none, mister."

"No?"

"No." He grinned, exposing yellowed teeth. "She's got one of her own."

I paid him and left. The red building was easy to find.

I rapped on the door twice with my knuckles, peering at the numerals in the dimness of the hallway. The door opened quickly, and the girl standing there almost fell out into the hall.

"Oh," she said. She put her hand to her mouth. "What is it?"

"Miss Blaney?"

"Yes. Yes, I'm Miss Blaney." Her voice was hurried, and she kept looking past me down the hallway.

"May I come in?"

"What for? I mean, what do you want?"

"I want to talk about Jerry."

"Oh." She put her hand to her mouth again, and then brushed a wisp of red hair off her forehead. "Jerry. Yes, come in. Come in."

The apartment was a shambles. Dishes were piled in the sink, and empty beer bottles cluttered the floor. The shades were drawn against the sun, and the bed at the far end of the room was unmade.

Claire Blaney glanced at the mess, and then pulled her faded silk robe tighter around her waist. She was a tall girl, with fiery red hair crowning her head, and arching eyebrows against a high forehead. Her deep-set green eyes were darting nervously, the way an addict's eyes will, never focusing on anything. Her slim shoulders dropped down to full, rounded breasts that moved gently when she walked, nudging the thin fabric of her robe. She had wide hips and long tapering legs. The robe was an old one, a little too short, ending just above the knee. It was tied at the waist with a dirty cord. Nothing else held it closed.

She took a cigarette from a crumpled package on the table, smoothed it out with her fingers and then thrust it between her lips. She wore no make-up, and her lips were pale and full, dry after a night's sleep. Her fingers trembled when she lit the cigarette.

"What about Jerry?" she asked.

"Where is he?"

"I don't know. Listen, are you going to ask me questions? If you're going to ask me questions, you can leave right now. I'm expecting someone."

"Jerry?"

"No."

"Who?"

"Someone."

"The Man?" I asked.

Her eyes opened wide. "What?"

"Honey, I've seen enough to know someone who's waiting for The Man. You haven't had your shot yet, have you?"

"Nobody asked you."

"When's he coming?"

She glanced at the clock on the wall. "He should have been here already. Damn it, where is he?"

She began to pace the room, her shoulders straight, her breasts moving rhythmically from side to side with each step she took.

"Why was Peter D'Allessio rubbed?" I asked.

"How the hell should I know?…Are you a cop?"

"No."

"How the hell should I know?" she repeated.

"What's Jerry got himself into?"

"What do you mean?"

"Nobody rubs a junkie's father just because he's going to the police. One junkie more or less doesn't mean beans to a pusher."

"So?"

"So why? Why kill the old man? I keep asking myself that."

"Go find out if you're so damned interested." She looked up at the clock again. "Where the hell is he?"

"He'll be here. Relax."

"He'd better be here. He'd better be here damn soon. Man, I'm overdue."

She crossed to the table and leaned over to put out her cigarette. Then she began pacing again. It was beginning to eat at her. It was beginning to get under her skin and crawl in her blood. I could see a fine film of sweat on her forehead. Her hands were really shaking now, and she kept pulling at the robe. She scratched at her head, then raked her long nails over the skin on her arms. She bit her lips, glanced at the clock again.

"Jeez, what's keeping him? What's keeping him?"

She walked to the bed and sat down. She got up almost instantly and began walking again. I watched her shivering violently, her teeth chattering now, her face looking as if it were ready to fall apart.

"Easy," I said. "Easy."

"Get out of here," she shrieked. "I won't have you watching me."

"Easy," I told her.

She walked to the table and reached into the crumpled pack for another cigarette. The pack was empty and she threw it away. I took out a cigarette and offered it to her. Greedily, she snatched at it, and I lit it for her while she continued to shiver.

She turned away suddenly and said, "I'm itchy. I'm itchy all over. Like bugs were on me. All over, crawling all over me."

She unloosened the cord at her waist and threw the robe open, exposing her hard, flat stomach, and the curving whiteness of her hips and thighs. She didn't care about me now. She only cared about the monkey who was tearing her shoulder to shreds. She ran to the bed and yelled, "God, God!", throwing herself forward onto the mattress. She wriggled frantically and her back arched high into the air, her leg muscles straining. She subsided in a sobbing heap and shouted, "Where *is* he? Where *is* he?"

Her back arched again, her breasts high, every muscle in her body quivering with the longing for the drug.

"Come here," she pleaded. "Do something. Do something for me. Do something. Do something."

I walked to the bed and stroked her body gently. She trembled violently, her breath raging into her lungs.

"Do something! Do something! Please, please, please."

I slapped her across the face. "Snap out of it," I said.

"Again, again. Hit me again. Please, please."

I hit her harder this time, and she moaned softly and reached up, throwing her arms around my neck. Her teeth clamped onto my neck, and she became a writhing, wriggling animal, her screams tearing across the room. I shoved her away and she flopped back onto the mattress, her eyes wide.

Nothing can help a junkie but the junk.

When I left her, she was still moaning on the bed, still crying for The Man who could put her out of her misery. On the way down, I passed a short, dark guy in a loud sports shirt, a package under his arm.

"You'd better hurry," I told him. "You're about to lose a customer."

He grunted and kept walking up the steps, looking back once to study my face more closely. I studied his face, too, and then I walked down to the ground floor. Instead of going out of the building, I went behind the steps and sat on one of the garbage cans there.

I waited for about fifteen minutes, and then I heard light steps coming down the stairs. When the steps reached the ground floor, I peeked out and saw the loud sports shirt drifting toward the front door. I gave him a chance to reach the street, and then I started after him.

With that shirt, you could have tailed him in a snowstorm. It was yellow and green, and it stood out like a beacon for foundering ships. I kept walking after him, quickening my pace when he did, never taking my eyes from the shirt. He turned a corner after we'd walked three blocks, and I ran to the corner, anxious not to lose him. I rounded the corner at a trot and walked right into the business end of a Colt .38.

"What is it, chum?" he asked. He had a thin, suspicious face with heavy brows and dark brown eyes. He sported a little mustache under his nose, and his teeth protruded over his lower lip.

"Put up the artillery," I said. "This is a friendly visit."

"I ain't got no friends, chum," he told me.

"Claire Blaney's one of your friends, isn't she?"

He kept the .38 leveled at my stomach. "What if she is a friend?"

"Is Jerry D'Allessio a friend, too?"

"What's your game, chum?"

"I want to know who killed Peter D'Allessio."

"Why?"

"I just want to know."

He pointed the gun downward suggestively. "You want to keep that, you better get the hell out of this neighborhood."

"That right?"

"That's right, chum."

I nodded. "Okay. Suits me fine." I started to turn away from him, and then I brought my right fist around in a short chop to his gut. He was about to trigger off a shot when I brought the edge of my left hand down on his wrist. He bellowed and dropped the gun, and I kicked it clattering across the sidewalk. I grabbed him then and gave him another hard right on his shoulder, bringing the edge of my hand down like a knife. He brought his shoulder up in pain, and his face screwed up into a tight knot.

"Where's Jerry?" I asked.

"I don't know."

I backhanded him across the mouth, and a spurt of blood appeared at the corner of his lips. "Junior, I'm not kidding. I almost killed a lot of guys, and I'm ready to go all the way with you. Where is he?"

"Wise up. I don't know."

"I'll wise up," I told him. I slapped him again, harder. "Where is he?"

"So help me, I don't know."

This time I gave him my fist, square in his mouth. He was spitting teeth when he finally decided to talk.

"All right, all right, I'll show you."

"This better be straight goods."

"The goods," he said. "The goods. Honest."

I picked his .38 out of the gutter and tucked it into my waistband. I shoved him ahead of me, and then we started out to find the junkie whose father had died.

The sports shirt left me outside a small door in a narrow alley. He pointed to the door, and then he took off like a big bird, his mouth still bleeding.

I lifted my hand and rapped on the door.

There was no sound inside, no light.

I tapped again.

"Yes, who is it?" a voice whispered.

"A visitor."

"Go away."

"Open up, D'Allessio," I said.

"Go away, damn it."

"You want it broken in?"

"Yeah, break it in. Go ahead, break it in."

I backed up to the opposite wall of the alley and shoved the sole of my foot against it. When my shoulder hit the door, it splintered with a rushing crack of old wood, and I stumbled into the room, fighting for balance.

I felt around for a light switch, finally located a pull chain. I yanked it, and a dim bulb splashed some feeble light into the small room.

D'Allessio was curled up against the wall, on the bed.

This wasn't the D'Allessio I'd seen in the wallet. The same

long nose was there, and the same pale eyes—but the face was thin, the skin pulled in tight under his cheekbones. His lips were bloodless, and his exposed arms bore the telltale scars of thousands of injections.

It was his eyes that told the whole story, though. They blinked like blind whirlpools in his head, the pupils large and black and staring. Haunted eyes. Eyes possessed of a ghost, a ghost named heroin.

"D'Allessio?" I asked.

"Who's the strong man? Who's the man goes around breaking doors?"

"Matt Cordell," I told him.

"Matt Cordell." He gave a low chuckle that died in his throat. "The disillusioned peeper." He chuckled again, huddled against the wall like a skinny pack rat.

"Your father wanted me to find you," I said. "That was before someone killed him."

"Yeah?"

"Yeah. He wanted me to find you so he could take you off the stuff. Your father had pipe dreams."

"Don't I know it!" He chuckled again, his teeth flashing in his gaunt face. "Shake the monkey? Like fun. Lexington, he said. Lexington, Kentucky. Man, he had rocks. That goddam penal colony?"

"They cure people there," I said.

"Sure, criminals. I'm no criminal."

"You are now," I said.

"What?"

"He was only trying to help you, Jerry. You had no reason to shoot him."

D'Allessio sat up on the bed, and his eyes were wider now, still staring, still lifeless. "You're off your rocker," he said.

"Who else? Cousin Marie? She's too busy. Claire? For what purpose? Hoss is everything to her, the way it is to you. Edith Rossi? She was trying to help you, and she knew your father was doing the same thing."

"You've flipped your cork, Cordell. Go break your way out of here. I'm sleepy."

"I thought maybe the pushers did it, but what for? You're dirt to them, Jerry. Dirt under their feet. Your father was a danger to only one person—the person he might've told the police about when I wouldn't help. You."

The gun came up from beneath the pillow before I could reach for the .38 in my waistband. D'Allessio held it steady, and he grinned over it, still lying full length on on the bed.

When he spoke, he spoke slowly, separating the two words. "So what?" he said.

"So nothing. Your father's going to cure you after all, Jerry. There's no better cure than the electric chair. That's the only permanent cure."

"And who's going to take me to the chair?" he asked.

"Me."

"Ha. Joke."

"Sure," I said, "me. I'm going to take that gun away from you in about three seconds, and then I'm going to make a citizen's arrest and cart you down to Homicide. Me."

"You must be tired of living," he said.

"That's it, friend, that's it exactly. I just don't give a damn, you see. You can shoot me but you'll get it anyway, and if you kill me, you'll be doing me a favor. Like a mutual friend said, I died a long time ago." I took a step closer to the bed. "Give me the gun, kid."

"Stay where you are," he shouted. He was sitting up now, his trousers rumpled over his knees, the needle marks showing on his legs, too, marks he'd killed to keep.

I walked up to the bed, holding out my hand.

His eyes were wide with fear, and his hand began to tremble. I watched the trigger finger, watched the skin grow white on his knuckle as the finger tightened.

"Give it to me!" I shouted.

For a second, I thought he was going to shoot. And then he threw himself full length on the bed, the gun clattering to the floor. He began crying, the sobs ripping into his chest.

"I'm no good. I'm no damn good," he said.

"You just took the wrong trolley, kid."

"My own father, my own father. I'm no good."

"Come on, kid," I said. "Come on."

He was still crying when I led him out of that dark alley into the sunshine that spilled onto the pavement. He didn't say a word when the Homicide boys took over. I gave them his gun and told them Ballistics would probably match the bullets in it with the ones found in Peter D'Allessio's body.

I didn't wait for thanks. I headed for the nearest bar.

I sat and drank, and I thought of the kid and whatever ghost had driven him to drugs and the murder of his own father. The ghost would stay with him right to the end. Ghosts die hard. I know all about ghosts.

I lifted my glass and I drank.